MEN BEWARE WOMEN

by

Gwen Thompson

Miami University Press
Oxford, Ohio

Edited by Margaret Luongo
Cover design by Madge Duffey
Page design by Dana Leonard

Library of Congress Cataloging-in-Publication Data

Thompson, Gwen B.
 Men beware women / by Gwen Thompson.
    p. cm.
 ISBN 978-1-881163-51-0
 1. Americans--England--Oxford--Fiction.
 2. Rowing--Fiction. 3. Shakespeare, William,
 1564-1616--Study and teaching--Fiction. I. Title.
 PS3620.H665M46 2012
 813'.6--dc23
                                    2012019183

Michaelmas Term 1990

MALCOLM KICKED OPEN THE DOOR TO HIS assigned room and saw that he would have to unpack in order to enter: there was not enough floor space for himself and his luggage. When he opened the closet door, it grazed the back of the desk chair. The slatted shelves inside were nailed down unfinished amid a network of hot water pipes and cotton-candy insulation; when he threw his clothes inside, they caught on splinters. He squeezed past the desk, tripped, and foresaw a year of barking his shins on the portable electric fire that was the only source of heat. A plain white bookcase was crammed in alongside the low single bed; a bare bulb dangled from the ceiling; there was nothing else. The walk-in closets in his mother's New York apartment were bigger.

The row house his room had been tacked onto as an afterthought was old by American standards:

worked into the diamond pattern of the gable, in contrasting colors of brick, was the year 1885. The neighborhood—six streets and two pubs—was an island ringed with canals, accessed by a humped stone bridge he'd crossed in the back of a big black cab with lots of leg room.

Jet-lagged, dehydrated, all he wanted to do right now was sleep, but the director of the foreign exchange program had invited new students to a welcome reception in a similar row house across the street. Her blonde hair was sprayed stiffly into place like a helmet, and her front room had a sweaty, tropical feel, with too many plants and wallpaper that emphasized pea green. There was a good deal of bad wine, and by the time it was gone, it seemed imperative to all present to take a moonlit stroll along the canal, down the muddy towpath winding into town; thus Malcolm's introduction to Oxford took place drunken in the dark. All he remembered afterwards was an Australian asking him for directions to Carfax.

"Tim, wasn't it?" Malcolm asked the slight, curly-topped young man who had the front bedroom.

"Yeh. Have you got any food in yet? I've another tin of beans, and bread for toast, if you haven't."

"I was thinking more along the lines of aspirin." The wine had been wretched, and he rarely bothered with breakfast.

"Oh, right. Should be some paracetamol over

the sink in the loo."

Once he'd tended to his head, Malcolm sat down at the kitchen table; blackened with age and grease, wood grain raised with scrubbing, it looked left over from another century. "Who's got the room next door?"

"Iranian chap. He was up and out early. Said something about Aikido. Where in the States are you from?"

"New York."

"I say, do you know—"

"No!"

Tim stared at him.

"Sorry," Malcolm said. "With eight million people, you get tired of the question."

"Righto." Tim spooned more beans out of the can onto his toast and revealed he was a second-year from Barrow-in-Furness and glad to have escaped it.

"Why? Where is it?"

"At the end of the longest cul-de-sac in the country," Tim told him. "Feels more like the end of the earth." He refilled his mug from the chipped teapot; the mug wore a Union Jack with the caption BE BRITISH BUY BRITISH. "I'm reading PPE. You?"

"What's PPE?"

"Philosophy, Politics, and Economics."

"Definitely not that! English Lit."

Tim nodded, swallowed the last of his breakfast, and got up to put his dishes in the sink. The sauce his beans were swimming in was red, not brown, and the Heinz label on the can was blue, not green. "Shall I tell you which are the cheapest supermarkets, or will you be eating in Hall?" he asked over his shoulder.

"In hall?"

"In college."

"I don't know. Is the food good?"

"Don't think I'd go so far as to say that—but it's cheap."

"Anything else I should know?"

"You'll need a bike, of course. Don't buy a new one unless you want it to get stolen. The ones at the police pound are the cheapest, but they tend to fall apart. Pennyfarthing's in George Street sell used ones in good nick, or you can hire one by the term. But if you're here for the year, it'll work out cheaper to buy one used and sell it back when you leave."

Now that he was sober, Oxford's orientation was self-evident: the two main drags ran east-west and north-south, crossing in the town center near Carfax Tower the Australian couldn't locate last night. There were pubs on every block—not just on the kinds of blocks where bars would be in the States—and Blackwell's bookshop, in its various incarnations, occupied most of Broad Street. Boots turned out to be a pharmacy, not a shoe store, and Lloyds could be either a bank or a pharmacy—which was called a chemist's. When Malcolm opened an account to deposit his travelers' checks, he was issued what looked like a credit card but behaved like an ATM card, and a checkbook with stubs instead of a register—something he'd read about but never seen. Yet he'd read so many books set here, England looked more or less as he'd imagined, the red buses, mailboxes, and phone booths familiar, not foreign.

Preparing for the academic year at Oxford entailed purchasing a collapsible Chinese paper lantern to shade the bare bulb in his bedroom; submitting twenty-seven passport photos to various organizations that wanted to keep tabs on him; registering as a resident alien with the Thames Valley Police; and signing his name to a statement in which he swore never to kindle any flame within the Bodleian Library.

When he blundered into the covered market in search of a sandwich, he found himself face to face with a row of dead rabbits hanging from the ceiling next to carcasses more difficult to identify—pheasants? Not so different from the headless ducks on display in Chinatown or the bloodied cobblestones in the Meatpacking District, but the air in England wasn't like air in America: damp and thick with scent like spring, it tugged him towards the brilliant squares of green glimpsed through the college gates. Unlike New York, Oxford's oldest buildings were biggest, the converse of skyscrapers funneling human energy inside to be intensified: each college quad—once you got past the porter—an oasis, its deep calm contagious.

On Friday in Noughth Week Malcolm rode a midnight-blue used Raleigh three-speed down the High to the Freshers' Fair in the Examination Schools; he hadn't seen a three-speed in America since mountain bikes took over, but here they still predominated. Making the rounds of the display tables and booths dwarfed by the cavernous, echoing halls seemed as good a way as any of examining the female freshers, so he wrote down his name and college on the mailing lists of a dozen Oxford societies with interesting-sounding names, and extricated himself from their less interesting-sounding representatives. When this proved tedious, he wrote down an assumed name and college to speed his getaway.

He could have spent every evening of the first two weeks of Michaelmas Term at a different freshers' drinks party sponsored by one student society or another in hopes of swelling their ranks, but after a blurry weekend of bops, settled down to concentrate on crew—which the English called rowing. Tryouts were not much different in England—how's your time on the erg, how far can you run, how fast, how many sit-ups and chin-ups and push-ups can you do before collapsing—and he was still fit from a summer spent sculling and playing tennis. Once he'd established himself as a serious contender for a seat in his college's first eight, the student societies' term cards and handwritten invitations that filled his pigeonhole in the porter's lodge got filed under the bed.

Malcolm's literature tutor had rooms in college overlooking the main quad, where the lawn, already a striped crewcut, was getting a trim from a man pushing a mechanical mower at a pre-industrial pace. Its rusty chirps were the only sounds within medieval walls thick enough to absorb and deflect the modern street noise outside. On his way round the perimeter, Malcolm counted four KEEP OFF THE GRASS signs and two Bulldogs who looked ready to enforce them. That must be the secret to Wimbledon, he thought. If there's one thing they get right here, it's grass. Did it glow like the Emerald City despite the cloud cover, or because of it?

The steps of the stone staircase were worn smooth and shallow in the middle from centuries of student feet. Malcolm knocked once, got no answer, and knocked harder. The door opened.

"Hullo—you must be Mr. Forrester?"

Malcolm glanced over his shoulder, half-expecting to find his father behind him, then realized his tutor was addressing him and shook his outstretched hand.

Professor Barraclough was a white-haired bear of a man whose Thursday wardrobe consisted of a blue checked shirt with one of the collar points turned up, a moth-eaten gray sweater, and dark woolen trousers in need of an iron. He ushered Malcolm in ahead of him. "Do sit down."

All the chairs were very low to the ground, and all the windows very high up the walls.

Professor Barraclough put on a pair of half-glasses and squinted down the full length of his arm. "I have a piece of paper here informing me you wish to study Shakespeare. Plays or poems?"

"Plays."

"Perhaps we had better establish straight away which ones you've read."

"All of them."

"Oh?" He raised his eyebrows. "No harm in reading them again."

"I know—I have."

"Secretly planning to be an actor, are you?"

"No. Don't have the face for it."

Professor Barraclough took off his reading glasses for a better look. "I should say you *had*."

"Facial expression," Malcolm said. "This is the only one I've got."

"Not terribly expressive as expressions go, is it?" Professor Barraclough set his glasses down atop a pile of desk debris they immediately slid off. "Presumably you've no objection to sitting in the audience?"

"No."

"Right." He clapped his hands together and stood up as the piece of paper fluttered to the floor. "We shall be sending you to London and Stratford, then, regularly. You can't have seen them all done live in the States, at any rate."

"No."

"Very well. You shall simply re-read whatever's currently playing and write your essays on that." He rested his hand on the one corner of the desk not buried under an impending avalanche of books and papers. "Are you equally familiar with Jacobean drama?"

"No. Once I got hooked on Shakespeare, I didn't want to read much else."

"Do you good, then. The Jacobeans are altogether different, and as it happens, there's a student company putting on Middleton in London at the weekend. Why not run up to Town for that as well?" He turned away to dig for something on his desk, then faced back round. "It's quite the funniest tragedy I've ever seen."

At *Women Beware Women* Malcolm laughed out loud, glad he hadn't spoiled the jokes by reading them beforehand. Students or not, the acting was superb, especially Bianca, who carried a calculated swivel in her step and a gaze of seraphic intensity down the full trajectory from innocence to corruption to remorse.

She's not even that pretty, he thought when he got a closer look during the curtain calls. All the more impressive. Then, What the hell? It worked for that Duke in the play, didn't it? He pushed his way against the exiting tide, checking the program for her name, and followed some people who looked like they knew where they were going through a side exit and down a dark, claustrophobic corridor toward the sounds of the cast undressing backstage.

"I say, where can I find Emma?" he asked the body next to him in his best British accent.

"Third door on the left," a gravelly voice answered. "Got a fag?"

"Sorry—don't smoke." He rapped on the door, then opened it.

Emma Beresford was already out of her costume and into street clothes, still swabbing off her makeup. "Who the bloody hell—"

"'Methinks there is no spirit amongst us...But what divinely sparkles from the eyes of bright Bianca; we sat all in darkness But for that splendour—'"

She dropped her sponge. "You don't mean to say you'd read the play before?"

"No. I will now, though. Good stuff."

"Yes, but you're not an actor—or at any rate, not a good one. You just said the line, you didn't look it."

"No, I'm not an actor. I've just got a good memory."

"God, what a waste—it takes me ages to learn lines!"

"Maybe because you do look them. That was brilliant how you foreshadowed Bianca's social elevation physically."

"You noticed, did you?" She reached up to release her hair from its smooth bun; it bounced down light brown and curly.

"Your duke was brilliant too. They all were."

"He's gay, you know."

"Of course he is."

"Do you care?" She glanced up at him sideways, and he was forced to revise his opinion of her looks.

"Do I care?"

"If you did, I could pass the word along that you'd inquired."

"No, nothing so complicated. I'm here to pay tribute to you. Any suggestions how to do it?"

"Well, you could take me round the corner for a pint, once I've got my face off. Have a seat, if you can find one."

She returned her gaze to the mirror, and Malcolm leaned against a conga drum draped with a ripped piece of textured olive-green velvet. He could see how it would come in handy having a pub round every corner.

"Odd play for a tourist to turn up at." Emma sponged at her eyelids. "I thought you Yanks were what's been keeping *The Mousetrap* running all these years."

"I'm not a tourist. I'm here for the duration."

"Of what?"

"The academic year."

"Here in London?"

"No, Oxford."

She raised a brush to her hair. "Have you got a name?"

"Unfortunately."

"Why? What is it?"

He told her, and she said, "What's so awful about that? I must know half a dozen Malcolms."

"I came to the right country, then. Does the corner pub serve anything besides beer?"

She turned and stared at him. "There's always cider."

"Yeah, what else?"

"Scotch, of course."

He shook his head. "Can't stand the stuff. Tastes like smoke."

"Or gin."

"There aren't enough ice cubes in all of England to make a decent gin and tonic."

She put the brush down. "Are you sure you're in the right country?"

The Flask and Serpent (or Flagon and Dragon, as Emma called it) was heaving with cast, crew, and audience. The young man behind the bar drew Emma a half-pint of lager before she asked for it. She told Malcolm, "I work here part-time. Handy for the theatre."

He slurped without enthusiasm at a pint of cider as Emma explained that the production was a collaboration between her drama school and a series of guest lecturers in literature. "They're fascinated with the Jacobeans and trying to raise awareness of them, because how many people go to plays at all these days, let alone antique ones—and if they do, it had jolly well better be Shakespeare, since him at least they've heard of, et cetera. But another part of the problem, as they see it, is that the Jacobeans don't read as well on paper. You've got to see them brought to life to appreciate them—hence the collaboration." She swallowed some beer. "I think it's a brilliant idea, since we're already doing loads of Shakespeare—which is fine, of course, except that the directors who've been at it for years are bored by now, so we get stuck enacting their far-fetched interpretations."

Malcolm was about to commiserate, when a smallish middle-aged man in tan corduroy, with terrible teeth and strings of dark hair combed across a ruddy forehead, squeezed himself between two of the high stools to place a freckled hand on Emma's shoulder. "Well, m'dear, I think it's clear enough now why Middleton has languished in relative obscurity as long as he has."

Emma's hazel eyes narrowed, and Malcolm found himself saying, "Funny how much the audience enjoyed it."

"Yes, there's no accounting for taste—or lack thereof."

"Surely anyone not lacking it can do better than that in the way of congratulations."

The man's nose wrinkled as if he were about to sneeze. "No doubt. However, I prefer to reserve them for when they're in order."

"Must get lonely up there on top of the mountain."

The man gazed impassively at him, as if he were a spider on the ceiling, then turned away. "Miss Beresford, who is this...creature? Or rather, who exactly does he think he is?"

"Never mind me," Malcolm cut in. "Who do you think you are, taunting Emma instead of toasting her? 'That wit deserves to be made much on!'"

The man looked him over again, then seemed to decide the bug was not worth swatting down and stepping on. "Indeed," he said. "Too bad the same cannot be said of yours."

He took himself off, and Emma said, "'I kiss thee for that spirit!'" And did—and how.

"Who was that?" Malcolm asked when he came up for air.

"One of my drama tutors. Are you always so spectacularly rude?"

"Only when it's in order." He grinned. "Why? Have I done something dire?"

Emma laughed into her glass. "If you have, it was worth it. His nose is out of joint because the literature tutors insisted on 'interfering' with the rehearsal process—but who cares, so long as they've got good ideas? He doesn't believe in anything but Brecht—all that outdated rot about alienating the audience. Everyone's already alienated nowadays—or too sophisticated to have fun. It probably took all his willpower not to laugh out loud along with everyone else."

Malcolm frowned. "That was the best thing about it! You can't help feeling for all the characters, even though they're all despicable. That's one better than Brecht."

Emma put her glass down. "'If I laugh at any mortal thing, 'Tis that I may not weep.'" She glanced at her watch. "They'll call time soon, but we can have another at my flat."

They had several, and the place to themselves.

Malcolm caught an early train back to Oxford the next morning, tripped over the milk bottles sitting out on the front step, and for the rest of Michaelmas Term spent a good deal of time on the Thames Line between Oxford and London. Traveling in the opposite direction from commuters, he usually found a free table at which to write his essays on the way to Town, or, coming home, an empty compartment in which to sleep.

After hitting the half-price ticket booth in Leicester Square, he spent the time till curtain-up browsing the used book stores in Charing Cross Road—the only shops in London with late opening hours. Sometimes he and Emma went to plays together; sometimes she stood on stage while he sat in the audience; sometimes, if she'd already seen a show he hadn't, he went on his own and talked to her across the bar at the Flagon and

Dragon afterwards.

"You've come a long way for a short drink," she said, handing him a shot of Irish whisky. "Last I heard, there was no shortage of pubs in Oxford—or have you got yourself chucked out of all of them already?"

"All the better ones." He didn't care how busy it was, or how long she could linger at his end of the bar between customers. Somehow it was possible to sit still in an English pub in a way it was not in an American bar, and he was happy just to watch her skim back and forth with pints of gold, black, and amber.

"So who is she?" Tim asked when Malcolm came in early one morning to grab a bite to eat and change clothes for rowing practice.

Today would be a steady-state workout, but erg tests loomed in the near future, and then seat-racing to select crews for Nephthys Regatta; hopefully rowing on either side—as Malcolm's high-school coach had insisted they all do—would double his chances of a seat in the first boat.

"If you try to tell me Jane Austen or Mary Shelley, I shan't believe you," Tim added.

"Mary Shelley? God forbid! What are you on about?"

"People who've been up all night in the library writing essays don't glow like that the morning after."

"Hell, no! I met a drama student in London."

"And?" Tim paused with a mug of tea halfway to his mouth. "Clearly you've done more than meet her."

"And she's really brilliant." Malcolm tossed some bread in the toaster. It was hard to keep a straight face when they told him at the bakery it would cost a penny more to slice it. "A brilliant actress." He dug some marmalade out of the dorm-sized fridge they all shared and sat down at the table. "We've been going to plays together. She never talks through them, but she has plenty to say once the curtain falls. Why is everybody else the opposite?"

The toast popped, and Tim said, "Whilst you're up, plug the kettle back in, will you?"

"Sure." Malcolm had no use for tea outside of Chinese restaurants, yet somehow the clouds of steam Tim generated every morning altered the atmosphere in the kitchen for the better.

"Is she pretty?"

Malcolm nodded, mouth full of toast. "'She doth teach the torches to burn bright.'"

"Come again?"

"You don't see anybody else when she's around—at least, I don't."

The tea kettle boiled and shut itself off, and Tim got up to refill the pot. English electric kettles didn't whistle with ear-splitting urgency; they bubbled, gurgled, and subsided of their own accord.

"Smart, too." Malcolm buttered more toast.

"We went to see Derek Jacobi in *Kean* at the Old Vic—more Dumas than Sartre, thank god—and you know what she said afterwards?"

Tim poured milk into his mug while the tea brewed in the pot.

"She said she hates playing existentialists, because what can you do with characters who don't do anything?" Malcolm spread on marmalade. He'd never liked it before, but it tasted better over here. "That's exactly what I've always hated about existentialism—it's as useless dramatically as it is practically."

"Just as well I've no set papers to do on Sartre, then." Tim mopped up his spilled beans with the last of his toast. He was clearly very smart, or he wouldn't be at Oxford, but he wasn't smart in the same ways as Malcolm; until Malcolm met Emma, neither had anybody else been.

"I guess you must be psyched that Mrs. Thatcher's stepped down at last," Malcolm said to Professor Barraclough as he shed his backpack and coat on Thanksgiving. He was not in the habit of paying much attention to politics, but Tim had had the BBC on during breakfast. Ever since his arrival at Oxford, Malcolm had been struck by the number of dons who got the same wistful, quixotic look in their eyes whenever the moribund Social Democratic Party was mentioned—while students allied themselves more pragmatically with Tory or Labour.

Professor Barraclough stopped short as he was crossing the room with a thick sheaf of galleys in hand. "What did you say?"

Malcolm made a quick mental check for Americanisms and recast his sentence. "I said, I suppose you're delighted with Mrs. Thatcher's resignation." Next thing he knew the galleys were flying up to the ceiling and fluttering down all over the floor.

"That's what I thought you said!" Professor Barraclough grabbed hold of both his hands and dragged him along in a circular, up-and-down dance round the room. When he'd finished jumping about, he asked: "Would you care for tea? No—sherry, I think, for the bearer of glad tidings." He let go of Malcolm to fetch and pour. "Here's to Heseltine!" They raised their glasses. "Though I haven't asked you," he said after a sip or two, "what you thought of Mrs. Thatcher's government. Perhaps you were among her supporters?"

"I think she's copied all of America's worst habits. Privatizing the world's greatest educational system, for instance. How does she think it got to be so great? Now no one can afford it. Though it's ironic that a country Americans consider so old-fashioned has had two female heads of state for so long."

"Old-fashioned? How so?"

"Still putting up with royalty, and the aristocracy, and a state church. Americans like to think we've moved beyond all that, but I'm not so sure."

"No?"

"We treat our President like royalty, not like an ordinary civil servant, and it's not as if we've got a classless society either. It's just that ours is based on money more than genealogy. But you can inherit wealth the same as a title, so how's that any nobler than nobility? Not to mention all the religious fanatics we've got in Congress—"

"As opposed to the bishops in the House of Lords, some of whom are atheists...well put. More sherry?"

It was good sherry from the college cellars, so Malcolm accepted several refills during the course of the hour and convinced himself he could decipher his handwriting more glibly as a result. At Yale papers were assigned with enough lead time to type them up; at Oxford—computers a rarity—essays were due each week, to be researched, handwritten, and read aloud. Until he sat there in the hot seat flipping through his notes to field his tutor's questions on the spot, Malcolm hadn't realized what a hurdle his handwriting was.

In Hall that evening they attempted a full Thanksgiving dinner for the benefit of the American students. Relieved to meet a menu that didn't center on stewed beef, Malcolm appreciated the gesture even though it didn't quite come off: mincemeat pie was no substitute for pumpkin, and it was impossible to convey how much Americans hate Brussels sprouts, because they seemed to be the official British vegetable for special occasions.

After dinner he rode over to the Radcliffe Camera to read the books he'd requested the day before. Taking notes in pencil took some getting used to, but it was that or adapt to fountain pens and the Bodleian's own ink that stained the long wooden tables fanned out around the circular reading room: ballpoint pens were banned. He finished just after nine and was bouncing over the cobblestones of Catte Street when Great Tom began to toll. He'd never stuck around to hear it sound all one hundred and one times, but the evening was clear and warm, so he circled down between the high stone walls of New College Lane into Queen's Lane, rode back up the High, and down St. Aldate's past Tom Tower, enjoying the breeze of motion. The foreign scents of burning coal and fermenting barley were oddly intoxicating, and the streets seemed livelier than usual, the pub crowds spilling out onto the sidewalks, still galvanized by the political charge in the air.

But next Thursday, when it was clear the mantle of power would not, after all, devolve upon Michael Heseltine as some had hoped and others feared, they were back to tea at his tutorials.

"So sorry, love!" Emma kissed him across the bar at the end of her afternoon shift. "They'd not got tickets to either of the plays you wanted to see at the booth in Leicester Square, and we can't go round my flat this evening, because both flatmates are determined to have their blokes in. I've tried begging and blackmail, but they won't budge."

"Did you try bribery?"

She shook her head, pulling him a pint of cider. "I'm skint as ever, but never mind. We can have tea—that is, supper—at my parents' instead."

"How is that an improvement?" Malcolm said, alarm bells ringing in his head.

"They'll feed and water us, for a start." She closed his fingers over his change.

"What are we, horses? There are such things as restaurants."

"I'd like to take you to dinner for a change."

"Oh." Emma had not previously struck him as the kind of girl who'd want him to meet her parents—had not, till now, owned up to having any.

"My sister can be a birk, but we have separate bedrooms."

Things were looking up. "Where do your parents live?"

"In Kent."

Malcolm tried and failed to remember where Kent was; it confounded him that English counties were so much smaller than American states. "Can I make it back to Oxford in time for practice tomorrow? The rest of the crew'll have it in for me if I'm late." Oliver Wells, the bow he'd displaced in his college's first eight, probably had it in for him already.

"I think so—I've got the timetable." She untied

her apron and came out from behind the bar. "Be sure to mention that's where you're off to."

"Why?"

"My parents still haven't forgiven me for going to drama school instead of university. I'm hoping to redeem myself by extension."

This struck him as a feeble excuse; she probably needed to fetch some things from home and wanted company on the train. "Let's see that timetable." Not exactly convenient, but doable. "I'll hardly get any sleep! You better keep me up all night so I don't mind."

"I think we'll manage." She reached around him for a sip of cider and pressed up close. "Dad snores so loud Mum wears earplugs."

Crammed into the southeast commuter rail, Malcolm recalled from a recent field trip that Canterbury was in Kent, and that Canterbury was near Dover, which was near France. "I don't see why we couldn't have gone to your flat. You've all got your own rooms. Can't you hang a bra on the doorknob?"

Emma looked blankly at him.

"Instead of a necktie. To signal you've got someone with you."

"Oh! Yes, but there'll still be masses of blokes about."

"Masses?"

"Well, two—but one of them..." She trailed

off.

"Yeah?"

"One of them used to be my bloke."

"So?"

"So one gets the impression you Yanks can be a prudish lot."

"You've been hanging with the wrong Yanks." The train was so crowded she had to sit on his lap—intoxicatingly close quarters.

The suburb where they disembarked resembled the outskirts of Oxford: long, low rows of brick and stucco buildings of an uninteresting age, the houses architecturally indistinguishable from the shops, without the dreaming spires in the distance to lend charm by association. Emma's mum greeted them at the door of a stucco terraced house identical to its neighbors and ushered them down a narrow, carpeted hallway into the living room—the lounge, she called it—with a barrage of questions as to what they could and couldn't eat, did or didn't drink, where they cared to sit till supper was ready, and when this might or might not be, depending on how it went with the roast in the oven.

Malcolm tried to convey that he was capable of eating and drinking most everything—not a vegetarian, not a teetotaler, no allergies, not overly concerned about mad cow disease—but found it hard to get a word in. He had not known having dinner guests could be so complicated; before they'd got as far as cocktails, Emma's mother had walked them through the pros and cons of all possible seating arrangements and gone on to explain, at some length, each course she proposed to serve. No doubt with the kindest of intentions, yet the onslaught of courtesy left him feeling he'd been bludgeoned with a blunt instrument.

Emma's parents seemed ancient to him, more like grandparents. Her mother wore old lady clothes in loud colors and had badly dyed hair; her father belted his trousers too high and sat slumped, an outgrowth of his armchair: when he stood up to shake hands, Malcolm half-expected to hear Velcro tear. Mr. Beresford seemed hard of hearing, but Malcolm soon suspected him of faking it in self-defense. Mrs. Beresford, concluding her spouse had grown more incompetent with age—she seemed the sort of woman who on principle assumed everyone else to be incompetent—fussed full-time, leaving her husband to stare at the telly and fiddle with drinks.

Malcolm was handed the inevitable glass of sherry, and during the lull while they raised their glasses, heard a stereo thumping dimly in the distance. Casting round for something to say, he noticed that the room was curiously devoid of ornament, its walls papered or plastered in a white, lumpy substance that bore a queasy resemblance to cottage cheese.

He caught Emma's elbow under cover of the

general shuffle from lounge to dining room. "Why does your mum keep explaining how we're going to eat dinner? Does she think I'm dim-witted?"

"No more so than anyone else." Emma rolled her eyes. "She just loves to fuss—you know what mothers are like."

Malcolm did not; the closest his mother came to fussing over him was to buy him, periodically, clothes he didn't need and wonder why he never wore them. "Not really—" He broke off, transfixed by the sheer ugliness of the carpeting: fuzzy floral shapes not so much curling as creeping, in shades of mustard, mushroom, and olive condensed to stale and soupy stickiness—colors no one could have chosen, that must have decayed to their current complexion. The tentacle-like tendrils drew his eyes up the steep staircase a pair of female legs were now descending: silver toenail polish, platform sandals, jeans glued on; striped stretchy top, scalding pink lips, extreme eye makeup, dark straight fringe.

The sum of these parts stopped dead on the landing to utter something that sounded like "Phwoar!" then hurtled the rest of the way down to teeter just short of crashing into them. Even with the psychedelic shoes she barely crested five feet.

"Meet my little sister, Chloe," Emma said without enthusiasm.

Chloe gave her a dirty look from underneath her bangs. "No need to rub it in, Em. Who's this, then? Not your American bloke?"

Emma nodded.

"Phwoar!" she said again. "Has he got a name?"

"Malcolm." He held out his hand.

"Delighted, I'm sure." She shook it and held on, blinking up at him through her smudgy eyelashes. "In fact, charmed."

"Mum says tea — supper's ready!" Emma hustled them along.

"In't he the spitting image of ——?" Chloe named some celebrity Malcolm had never heard of—and of whom she was deeply enamored, judging from her reverent tone of voice and the sidelong glances she kept shooting at him.

"That's enough of that, Chloe." Mrs. Beresford's diction was painfully precise. "He'll think all you ever do is read *Hello!*"

"Well, it is, innit?" She winked at Malcolm, then winced; Emma must have kicked her underneath the table.

"Have some more sprouts, why don't you, Chlo?" Emma mounded them onto her sister's plate.

"Slag!" Chloe mouthed at her, hurrying the serving dish along. "You look just like him," she insisted.

"Thanks," Malcolm said, "but I have no idea who that is."

She stared suspiciously at him from beneath her overgrown fringe. "You're just taking the piss out of me!"

"Chloe!" her mother interjected.

"Don't you ever watch telly?"

"Don't have one."

"Or films?"

"I prefer plays."

"What with all these Hollywood fan mags, you'd think all you Yanks ever did was swot up on your film stars' sex lives, innit?" She put her fork down halfway to her mouth, finding she'd been about to bite into a brussels sprout. "D'you reckon it's because you could all stand a good shagging in real life?"

"Chloe, will you please stop speaking like a guttersnipe!"

"Ew yes, one must speak vedy, vedy properly, even if one hesn't been to univarsity!" She giggled at the sound of her absurdly upper-crust vowels.

Mr. Beresford went on spreading horseradish thickly over his sliced beef, having mentally seceded from his family some time ago.

"You can't have it both ways," Malcolm told Chloe. With all that makeup, it was hard to tell how old she was. "The American girls I've met over here complain that British guys think they're all easy."

"Well, it *is* all we ever think about here!" Chloe grinned and flicked her fringe aside.

"It most certainly is not!" Mrs. Beresford put down her knife and fork in protest.

Chloe shrugged and rolled her eyes.

Emma glared at her sister. "How's the food at

Oxford, Malcolm?"

"Mostly potatoes."

"Just as well I didn't go to university, then." She eyed her mother's well-upholstered figure. "I'd be as big as a house."

"Hasn't had that effect on him, has it?" Chloe countered.

"Well, he rows all the time, doesn't he?"

Malcolm, bored by the bickering, was thankful to be an only child who seldom ate with either of his parents, if this was what family dinners were like. "That's the fun part." He sawed at the gray beef. "Then there's all the running, lifting, and crunches we have to do besides."

Chloe made a face of disgust. "Won't catch me messing about with that rubbish—games mistresses are all lezzies!"

Emma stabbed a brussels sprout with her fork, then stabbed it again.

"Sorry about that." Emma took the stairs two at a time. "Can't get a word in edgewise when Chloe's about."

"Why'd you want to come, then?" Malcolm asked her.

She shrugged. "Free meal, isn't it?"

The spare bedroom looked as if a florist's had imploded, splattering wallpaper, curtains, lampshades, and the fluffy quilts Malcolm had learned to call duvets. There seemed no rhyme or reason to what matched and what didn't; even the bathroom walls were overgrown with flat floral arrangements laminated in unlikely pastels at the convergence of every four tiles. "Doesn't it give you a headache?" he asked Emma through a mouthful of toothpaste.

She shook her head. "Didn't catch a word—hurry up and spit, so I can kiss you good night!"

This was cut short by her mother's appearance at the foot of the stairs. "I'm so sorry, dear," she called up to Malcolm. "I didn't think to ask if you'd like a hot milky drink to take up with you?"

"A wha—I beg your pardon?"

"A hot milky drink to take to bed with you."

"Uh . . ." There was one thing Malcolm wanted to take to bed with him, but it was not hot milk; in his experience nightcaps were drunk before bed, not in it.

"Cocoa, Malcolm," Emma translated. "She means, do you want some cocoa?"

"Not necessarily, dear." Mrs. Beresford glossed over the impatient edge in her daughter's voice. "We've also Ovaltine or Horlicks, if he'd rather."

Malcolm had seen Tim on occasion stirring up something that smelled like baby formula and turned out to be Horlicks; he figured Ovaltine was likely to be more of same. "I already brushed my teeth."

Emma and her mother both stared blankly at him; no wonder the English had such terrible teeth! "I mean, no thank you."

Malcolm had thought his room in Oxford impossibly small, but the bedrooms in Emma's parents' house were not much larger, the furniture mismatched and nondescript, jammed against walls and crammed into corners. He switched the light off to tone down the flowers, and was half undressed when the door opened and Chloe entered, wrapped in a candy-striped robe several sizes too big, hair slicked back wet.

"Oh, sorry!" She flipped the light on. "Wrong room."

"This is your house!"

She shrugged and shut the door behind her. "I had to ask when Emma's not around: are you really an American?"

Malcolm stared at her. "Why would anyone pretend to be American?" Particularly during the Gulf War.

"Prove it, then! Talk about baseball." She put her hands on her hips.

"I don't follow baseball."

"Which sports do you follow, then?"

"Rowing. Tennis."

"Those could just as well be British."

"Not all Americans like baseball. Some people think it's so boring they watch American football instead."

Chloe made a face. "Rugger for poofs, that is! Fancy wearing all that armor to do sport!"

"You could look at it that way," he agreed. "Or

you could look at rugby as an excuse for a bunch of guys to roll around in the mud together."

Chloe sniggered at this. "Tell me about your armored rugby, then."

"I don't follow that either. It's more boring than baseball—almost as boring as cricket."

"Right," she conceded, "I reckon you really are American if you're up at Oxford and hate cricket. Shame about the ten quid, though."

"What ten quid?"

"Emma didn't tell you?" A calculating look crossed her face.

"Tell me what?"

"About our wager. She told me she'd pulled this gorgey American bloke who looked just like ——" here she named the same movie star Malcolm had never heard of "and of course I didn't believe her, so she said, put your money where your mouth is, but I told her I wouldn't cough up till I saw him in the flesh. I reckoned you were just a mate from drama school who could fake the accent."

"No," he said, "British actors always fake Midwestern accents. I don't use that many Rs in a month."

"Sod it! I'm out a tenner, then. Speaking of flesh..." She bent her head over the belt to her bathrobe, then flashed him full on. "Bear this in mind, won't you? My room's next door." She spun around and departed.

Malcolm still had the after-image on his eyelids when he got into bed. Before his head hit the pillow, there was a knock at the door.

"Lost again?" he said, in case it was Chloe.

"A pen?" Her mother's voice came back at him. "No, I'm afraid I haven't—won't take a moment to fetch one."

As her voice receded, Malcolm grabbed his jeans and rifled the pockets for a piece of paper to make this unintentional request more plausible, but he needn't have bothered.

Mrs. Beresford handed him both pen and paper when she returned, and set a steaming floral mug down on a floral coaster. "I thought I'd better bring you up a hot drink after all, in case you got cold in the night. There's an extra blanket in the cupboard, and if you should need anything else...?"

"I'm fine, thanks."

The milky mixture in the mug smelled suspiciously like Horlicks, so Malcolm waited till her footsteps faded before pouring it out the window. British windows had no screens; he hoped when summer came, there'd be no bugs.

He'd turned the light off and nearly fallen asleep when the door opened again and somebody slid into bed beside him. "Emma?"

"Who the hell were you expecting, my mum?"

"She's already been. Brought me some horrible sweet drink. I dumped it out the window."

"Right into the hydrangeas! Well, you'll be long gone by the time she sees it." She started wriggling out of her pajamas.

"You sure we won't be disturbed?"

"I told you, Mt. Vesuvius could erupt in here and my parents would sleep through it."

"What about your sister? She—"

"Good point—she's the sort to burst in with a camera and take snaps. We'll have to prop a chair against the door." She sprang out of bed. "Only we'd better test this to be sure it works. I'll go out and try to get back in."

Malcolm got up, shoved the chair against the door, and leaned on it.

"That's brilliant, love!" Emma whispered from outside. "I can't shift it."

He let her in and propped the chair in place again.

She surveyed the result. "If anyone should come along, how will you explain the barricaded door?"

Malcolm thought this was beside the point. "How will you explain what you're doing here?"

"I shan't—I'll hide in the cupboard," she said, as if this happened often. "What about the chair?"

"I'll tell them New York's so dangerous, we all sleep with a chair shoved up against the door."

"So clever!" Emma smiled as she turned off the light, and Malcolm saw the afterglow of her teeth in the dark. "Were you clever enough to bring condoms?"

"What kind of a fool do you take me for?" He reached into the pocket of his jeans, which he'd flung over the chair, and threw one at her.

"What if you'd got hit by a bus? Think of your

poor parents when they received your personal effects."

Malcolm thought his father would be pleased he'd taken his advice to heart. "We'd better use them, then, in case I get hit by a bus going home."

"No worries, love." She reached under the mattress. "I'm a clever girl too."

"How are you going to spend the ten pounds?" Malcolm asked Emma before dawn, as he was getting dressed.

"Ten pounds?"

"Yeah, do I get a cut?"

She let out a hiss of annoyance. "Chloe ratted, did she?"

"Uh-huh."

"Silly tart! She can afford to lose bets, living home. Sorry you got caught in the middle, love. I get so sick of her prying, I just wanted to shut her up. She gets bored here—sneaks up to Town and mucks about backstage making a pest of herself. High time she got some boyfriends of her own!"

"Maybe she's planning to."

"What do you mean?"

He grinned. "Depends how much of a cut I get."

"Oh, go row your boat!" She gave him a shove in the direction of the door. "You'll miss your train if you don't get a move on!"

The hydrangea skeletons outside glowed ghostly

in the pre-dawn gloom. Malcolm turned to wave goodbye to Emma watching from the bedroom window—and saw another hand wave back from the window next door.

Malcolm loved the smell of the slow-moving Isis and the light reflected greenly off it; the rhythm of contracting then extending as a unit; so much strength, so little sound from the quick slice of blades through water. Pieces like today's when they stayed so in synch the shell seemed to skim above the river's glassy surface made up for the wet weather when oars slipped, blisters burst, and a headwind blew technique to bits as they pulled against waves and the weight of water that would drench them when they flipped the boat overhead to put it on the racks.

On the way home from practice, walls, gates, and railings were plastered with posters for Drama Cuppers at the Burton-Taylor Theatre. He stopped by the train station to call Emma from a card phone; the 3, 6, and 9 on the rotary payphone in his flat were so unreliable he ran out of change dialing wrong numbers.

"I don't think I can make it, love," she said. "I've got to—"

The arrival of the next train to Paddington drowned her out.

"What?" he said. "I can't hear you."

"I said, I'm horribly busy. There's—"

The final boarding call blared out: . . . calling at . . . Didcot Parkway . . . Slough . . .

"Can't you make time somehow?" he shouted over the din. "I've been down to London dozens of times, and you haven't come up to Oxford once."

"I know, love, it's just that—"

The PA system confirmed the London train's departure; Malcolm waited for it to finish before he went on in a normal tone of voice: "I don't know if I'll get to Town again before the end of term, and then I'll be off Eurailing for a month."

"My heart bleeds," Emma said. "Not much, though—I'll be in New York."

"The one Christmas I won't be! What for?"

"One of our tutors is delivering a lecture on Middleton at your Columbia University in December and has arranged for us to stage *Women Beware Women* there in conjunction with it."

"That's fantastic! Why didn't you tell me before?"

"I didn't want to jinx it—we weren't sure we'd get the funding."

He watched the units tick away on his phone card. "You know, my flatmates aren't around much more than yours are."

Silence.

"We don't even have adjacent bedrooms. Two floors in a terraced house."

More silence.

"Emma? Are you still there?"

"Yes, but—" A train from Reading arrived

through her answer. "...can't afford to...see what I can manage...Bye."

"What are you so happy about?" Emma asked him as the train pulled out. She was wearing a black skirt and gray sweater, but he'd spotted her immediately on the platform despite the drab colors. She stood still with as much controlled energy as the swarm of people around her expended rushing back and forth.

"I'm glad you could come." He kissed her hello.

"And?" She kissed him back.

"And what?"

"What else are you happy about?"

"Our boat did well in the Isis Winter League, and the Fairbairn Cup's coming up at Cambridge—"

"You're turning into a regular boatie, aren't you?"

"That's nothing new. I haven't rowed on starboard side since high school, but it's like riding a bicycle."

They walked towards the city center past Morrell's Brewery and down Paradise Lane, skirting the Castle Mound and Her Majesty's Prison to pass under the Westgate Shopping Center, then cut through Turn Again Lane to Rose Place and round the corner to The Elizabeth in St. Aldate's.

"I thought we'd eat before the show, and I'll show you round the flat later."

When the maître d' had seated them and dissolved into the dark woodwork, Emma whispered, "What's all this? When you said dinner, I thought you meant pub grub."

"Be a busman's holiday for you, wouldn't it? This place is supposed to be good."

"It had better be." She glanced at his menu; hers had no prices. "I don't spend this much on food in a week."

Malcolm looked it over. "Doesn't seem that bad compared to New York. I guess I'm used to it."

"Well, I'm not." She closed her menu. "I didn't bring that much dosh with me."

"That's OK. I brought plenty."

She opened the menu again. "Enough for wine?"

"Of course."

"What's the occasion?"

"No occasion. I just like wine."

She smiled. "What luck! So do I."

Half a bottle later, as they were finishing their pudding, Emma said, "That was miles better than pub grub—hope it doesn't break the bank! Do you come here often?"

"Never. I usually eat in Hall—takes the least time away from rowing. Too bad the food's not as impressive as the architecture. They don't even give you paper napkins. Once I asked the guy sitting next to me how he managed, and he said he used his sleeve."

The waiter brought the check, and Emma watched with a waitress's eye as Malcolm counted out the tip. His American wallet was not sized to accommodate pound notes whose size corresponded to their value, and the top edges of the larger bills were torn and crumpled.

"If that's how you usually tip, I wish you'd eat where I work."

Malcolm ended Emma's tour of the flat in his bedroom. "Did you get everything you had to do in London taken care of?"

"More or less." She turned away to examine the only window, corrugated bathroom glass you couldn't see into or out of.

"What were you so busy with?"

She shrugged, running her finger up and down one of the grooves, then faced him. "Where'd you get that black hair, anyway?" It tended to fall into his eyes, and she reached up to brush it back.

"From my mother. And my grandmother."

"Do Dark-Eyed Sailor eyes run in your family too?" Her hand landed on his shoulder.

"Only one pair per generation." He tried to pull her closer, but she grabbed his wrist.

"You're a washout as far as the lily-white hands, though." She fingered his rowing calluses, in a different configuration now that he'd switched from stroke side to bow side.

"Whoever heard of a sailor with lily-white hands?" He closed his around hers.

"I do know where you got your nose, though." She touched hers to his. "Tweaked it right off

David in Florence, you did."

"I mostly notice his hands—how you can see all the veins and tendons. Must be why Michelangelo made them so huge—"

Emma laughed. "Only they don't correspond to his—"

She broke off in a shriek as he tickled her, then lunged at him. They collapsed onto his bed, and he kicked the door shut—one advantage of the close quarters.

Emma ended up on top; after they'd exhausted themselves, the Chinese lantern swam back into focus over her shoulder. "You know who you look like?" he told her. "Whoever you're playing."

She made a sound that could have been surprise or pleasure. "Next time you see him, tell *David* he can't have his nose back—nor can he borrow any bits of yours."

CHRISTMAS VACS 1990-91

FOREWARNED BY A GUIDEBOOK WRITTEN ON THE assumption that everyone did their Grand Tour in summer, Malcolm arrived at the Galleria dell'Accademia in Florence before it opened, expecting to wait in line for several hours. Instead, he had the place to himself. *David*'s hands were even more outsized than they appeared in his art history textbook; he bought a close-up postcard to send Emma.

In the Convento di San Marco he discovered why everyone else did their Grand Tour in summer, as the bitter chill of the monastic cells where Fra Angelico painted Côte d'Azure-blue murals seeped into his bones, and with it the worst cold he'd had in years. The long queues of chain-smokers in Italian train stations didn't help; by the time he hit Rome, the tour guide in Keats' house edged away from him as if the poet's consumption might still be contagious a hundred fifty years later. He reached France with a fever, unfit to digest festive foie gras for Christmas and New Year's in Paris, choking down instead chalky throat lozenges and little green pills the *pharmacienne* claimed would disengage the coughing mechanism in his brain. (They didn't.) Recovered, he spent the rest of his holidays skiing at Zermatt with friends from high school and walking across where the Berlin Wall used to be.

Hilary Term 1991

WHEN HE GOT BACK TO ENGLAND, STILL SLIGHTLY queasy from the boat-train heaving towards the white cliffs of Dover, there was a pile of mail awaiting him on the kitchen table.

"Those overseas envelopes always look so much more interesting than ordinary tan ones," Tim observed, munching on a cheese and pickle sandwich as Malcolm slit one open.

> *Hello love,*
>
> *You'll never guess what's happened! I faked a fever to skive off breaking down the set, then snuck out of my 'sick-room' to an audition—and landed the bit Brit part in Through the Wringer Off-Off Broadway. It's not much, but it's paying, so I'm staying.*
>
> *Emma xx*

There was no return address. Malcolm stared down at the letter without seeing it. Then stared up at Tim without seeing him either.

"What?" said Tim. "Have I got pickle in my teeth?"

"No, I like your sweater." He felt like he'd been kicked in the stomach.

"It's my Christmas jumper."

"Christmas jumper?" Too late, he realized he'd started a conversation.

"You know, a Christmas jumper. Don't you get jumpers for Christmas?"

"No." What he got for Christmas were five-figure checks that had to be deposited before New Year's because of taxes.

He went to practice the next day in a daze, dimly aware of the cox and captain debating the merits of defying the rain and stream conditions. Out on the river he pulled as if they were doing sets of power tens. When he felt the telltale tug on his slippery oar, there was only a split second to decide what to do, and he didn't make allowances for heavy weather. Too late he tried to flatten out before the wave rose up, the blade dropped down, and the oar plowed into his side with all the momentum of eight twelve-stone men and a coxswain surging forward at fifteen miles an hour—which flattened him sure enough.

"Two broken," the Pakistani NHS doctor said, meaning Malcolm's ribs.

"You're kidding, right?" It hurt almost as much to talk as it did to breathe.

The man blinked at him. "No, I am not. You must take it easy for a couple of months to give the bones time to knit."

"A couple months? I'll miss Torpids!"

"Would you like to miss Eights as well?" The doctor's polite singsong sounded like an invitation. "Because that is what will happen otherwise. Ribs must be kept immobilized to heal properly." He wrapped Malcolm in an ace bandage and handed him a list of deep-breathing exercises and a prescription for painkillers to go with them. "Doing these will hurt like hell, but you must do them anyway, or you will lose some lung function and risk pneumonia."

Cringing through each day in constant expectation of unpleasantness—and getting it—Malcolm now understood his arthritic grandmother's reliance on scotch for medicinal purposes. He was used to drinking for pleasure, not pain, and was surprised how much it took to reach numbness. It did not make him feel any better to learn that his eight had been fined a hundred pounds by the University Rowing Clubs

Committee for disregarding the Red Flag the boat had slipped past during the chaos he'd caused catching a crab.

Tracing Emma proved easy enough: if she was going to be an actress, she would need a phone line in Manhattan. In fact, she had an answering service, but she didn't answer his messages, nor the letters he sent once he'd got her address from her flatmates—who were unfazed by her not writing it on the only envelope she'd sent him; in England no one bothered with return addresses.

Suddenly, without crew, and without Emma, there were five or six extra hours in each day. He had not appreciated how crew kept him on course: without that anchor, time tossed him about uncontrollably. In the library, in no hurry to get to practice, books he didn't need to read led him astray on his way to fetch the ones he did: lesser-known Victorian thrillers by Wilkie Collins, obscure and insignificant early works of Byron, Rose Macauley novels with their sexless protagonists. When practice would have ended, with no train to catch to London, he succumbed to authors absurd to read in England—Fitzgerald, Salinger—or stayed up all night mired in Somerset Maugham.

Even the ancient leather-bound tomes chained down in Duke Humfrey's Library lost their allure. Penciled glosses inscribed by past students, all but invisible, were often more illuminating than the texts themselves; and the unfathomable organization, in a subject as straightforward as English literature, seemed unconscionable. The family-Bible-sized volumes of the Bodleian's general catalogue were indexed only by author and date of publication; their manila pages ruled into thirds and numbered in faint pencil were rife with blank spots where the fortune-cookie slips of paper pasted in for each book appeared to have fallen out and never been replaced. Then there was the two-hour wait for any of the five million books to be retrieved from eighty miles of underground stacks. When he rode past the Old Bodleian on his bike, he could smell the dry rot wafting up through grates in the street. No wonder they held "Reader Services Surgeries"—these were just help sessions, but to American ears sounded sinister.

The underwater gloom filtering through the alabaster walls of Beinecke at Yale seemed like Paradise Lost in comparison. Duplicate copies of any books safely entombed in its central, climate-controlled glass tower could be checked out of Sterling and taken home to be used and abused for a whole semester, even if they were old enough to be bound in calfskin and printed on vellum.

Sometimes he tried to study in the Oxford Union Society's library; it wasn't the most up-to-date collection, but this hardly mattered for English lit. Here at least there were open stacks and a card catalogue of sorts: crumbly cards with faded brown ink in spiky old-fashioned script difficult to decipher. It was faster finding books here than in Bodley, but he didn't like to linger in the pre-Raphaelite reading room with its dirt-darkened decorations, creaky stairs and balconies, gray men in gray suits wedged into decaying leather armchairs. Were these the same old codgers snoring over their newspapers from one day to the next? For all he knew, they could've died and been rotting there for weeks.

He'd spent so much of Michaelmas Term in London's West End, he knew the ice cream flavors sold in each theatre at the interval by heart, but it was no fun to eat ice cream alone. When he retrieved the student societies' term cards from under his bed and flipped through them for something to do instead, their suggestions seemed absurd: *Talk in Ashmolean Museum on 'Neolithic Narcotics'... Don't just get drunk, come say L'Chaim... All you'll need is a change of underwear & T-shirt to explore the tightest caves in the country... Interested in learning to use Dark Ages weapons and carrying your skills into battle?... We go out every Saturday and most weekdays to stop the seven foxhunts, nine hare courses, and one minkhunt that operate throughout Oxfordshire... Want to throw yourself out of a plane? Do it for Rag and it becomes inexpensive... Squobbing, scrunging, nurdling, and more; you haven't lived if you haven't winked... Gwerddon gartrefol a CHYMDEITHAS ORAU'R BRIFYSGOL!!!*

He threw the leaflets back under the bed and

made the rounds of college bars and bops instead, where he tried to forget Emma and meet Oxford women, but they weren't real; he seemed to look through them, as if they were meaningless pixels of light on a screen. Was it his imagination, or did British women have unnaturally high voices? As did British men—or was it Americans who pitched their voices too low? The more he'd had to drink, the further his accent drifted across the Atlantic.

Beer and cider cost less in the college bars; much more logical—and convenient—that all students were of age in England, not just seniors. But there were all the same exaggerations of dress on display as at home, only grubbier: even the thick haze of cigarette smoke and the fog machine in the JCR could not conceal the insufficiencies of English plumbing when it came to bathing. Cycling home in the small hours to the buzz of the back-wheel generator powering his bike's headlight—faster past the kebab vans' off-putting odors—George Street was alive with townies immune to the weather: in micro-minis and deep necklines, they stood about waiting for the fights to finish up outside the rougher pubs at closing time.

He went pub-crawling for variety, and discovered, branching out from lager, that warm British beer had flavor. He didn't notice, between pints of bitter, whether he enjoyed himself or not; what kept him at the bar in the face of prowling cats and flying darts was the irony that in a book would be artistic but in real life rankled like a splinter: New Yorker in England falls for English girl who decamps to New York. He didn't know if Emma was deliberately ignoring him, or couldn't afford overseas phone calls, or if the address he had was only temporary, and she'd since moved on. Time passed, but her absence remained as jarring as the blackened statue of Queen Anne over the gates of Univ shaking her raised fist at him as he rode up the High.

His essays during Hilary Term didn't get written till the last minute, even though he had more time to write them; with nothing else to make time for, there seemed no reason to start sooner. When the pubs closed at eleven, he went home to make some headway on the week's impossibly long reading list, drifting off to the Shipping Forecast and "God Save the Queen" as Radio 4 went off-air for the night. Or, if he had an essay due the next day, let himself into the college library with his key and spent the rest of the night there—by no means the only student to do so. This was a safe enough strategy: if he nodded off before morning, the cleaning staff vacuuming at four or five a.m. were sure to rouse him. He'd never found getting up at the crack of dawn for crew anything other than agonizing, but staying up all night did not sit well either, no matter how late he slept in.

Whatever he wrote was well-written, regardless of substance; at home this had passed muster with overworked TAs relieved to be burdened with one less undergrad in need of coaching on punctuation and grammar. Squinting through his tutorials, he wondered if it was true that handwriting deteriorated under the influence—or if he could barely read his own because his eyes were so blurry the morning after.

He had no idea if it was day or night when he woke up; it took him a while to realize the pounding wasn't all inside his head, but coming from outside as well—his bedroom door, in fact. He sat up slowly and wished he'd sat up slower; luckily the room was so small there wasn't far to go to reach the door. He opened it to find both flatmates poised outside. "How come you're not at the library?" he asked Hadi, who spent so much time there and so little at home, Malcolm had half-forgotten what he looked like.

"We were hoping you could tell us what this means." Hadi handed him a small green slip of recycled paper torn from the pad kept by the phone for messages.

Malcolm forced his eyes to focus on what looked like it might possibly have been his own handwriting in about third grade: *Tim, Yecuda talled.*

"Is that for me?" Tim said. "Who's this Yecuda?"

Hadi asked, "And what is 'talled'?"

Malcolm kept staring at the paper, but it didn't make any more sense. "Beats me."

"You did write it, though?" Tim said. "Because

we didn't."

"Guess I must have. I remember the phone rang—woke me up—didn't think I'd reach it in time."

"But you did?" Hadi prompted.

"Yeah, only I couldn't understand the guy."

"So it was a man." Tim seized the salient point. "Are you sure it was for me? I don't know anybody called Yecuda—never heard the name before. Sounds foreign—perhaps you misspelt it?"

Malcolm couldn't think of any other names that sounded like Yecuda except Yehudi, and the only Yehudi he'd ever heard of was Yehudi Menuhin, who seemed an unlikely person to be ringing Tim. "I think," he said, struggling to recall the conversation he'd only been half-conscious for, "I think he asked who lived here...and when I told him, he said, 'Tell Tim'...or maybe 'Tell him...'"

"Do you know anybody called Yecuda?" Tim asked Hadi.

Hadi shook his head.

Malcolm squeezed his eyes shut against the bright light in the living room, but this only helped his headache, not his memory. "I'm sorry, that's all I remember. He said, 'Tell him'...or 'Tell Tim...Yecuda called' and hung up before I could ask him how to spell it, so I tried to sound it out..."

"Hang on!" Tim grabbed the piece of paper back from him. "I see what happened. What you just said isn't the same as what you wrote—you've reversed the sounds. 'Yecuda talled' must be 'Yetuda called'—you've spelt it in American, that's all."

"Come again?"

"'Your tutor called,'" Tim enunciated very slowly and clearly, with no trace of either R.

"Now we have only to determine whose tutor it was." Hadi looked pleased with the outcome.

"Hopefully not mine." Malcolm wasn't sure what day it was, let alone what time—near midday from the strength of sun blasting his eyes.

Tim stood in the kitchen toasting a cheese sandwich, wondering why he could never make them come right like his mum's did. True, his mum's frying pans were not as scarred and misshapen as this one which had with good reason been abandoned by a previous tenant. But he sometimes wondered if there wasn't a certain piquancy added by his mum's habitual grumbling at what it cost to heat the cooker just to toast a sandwich; he was about to apply this technique himself, when his American flatmate drifted in like something washed up with the tide. Since Malcolm had, on occasion, expressed frank incredulity at European practices—some British, some Continental—of charging extra to chill your drink or put ice in it, to slice your bread or butter it, to heat your pie or toast your sandwich, Tim postponed the experiment.

"Have a sandwich?" he offered, but Malcolm shook his head and shuddered. Just as well, given that Tim was running out of cheese. He wondered why Malcolm didn't go back to bed and sleep it off, instead of perching on an unforgiving wooden chair to stare down at the table, elbows boring into the woodgrain, knuckles gouging his temples as if to relieve the pressure with a puncture. No one expected students to keep reasonable hours, unless they had morning tutorials, which fortunately Malcolm hadn't this term, or Tim didn't see how he could've gone on as he did: eventually, after ten or fifteen minutes' meditation on the unresponsive tabletop, gathering the resources to get up and make a cup of instant coffee, complain it tasted foul, and drag himself off to the Bodleian to write his essay in the few hours before the pubs reopened. Tim couldn't fathom how he got by spending so little time at it, hung-over besides.

He switched off the stove and sat down with his sandwich, burning his fingers; he generally didn't bother with plates, as there was less to wash up afterwards. "Whatever happened to that bird of yours in London?" he asked through a mouthful of melted cheddar.

"Moved to New York."

"Seemed like you spent half your time at hers last term—must be a bit of a blow."

"Yeah, a bit."

Tim wasn't sure what to make of this. "Thought you were getting on like a house afire."

"So did I."

"Gave you the push, did she?"

Malcolm tore his eyes away from the crumbs on the tabletop, some fresh and some of ancient vintage. "I don't know what happened. She won't return my calls or answer my letters."

"Maybe you should go to an island," Tim suggested.

Malcolm stared at him. "This whole country's an island—so's this neighborhood." He brushed off the crumbs stuck to his elbows. "I've lived my whole life on islands: Manhattan in the winter, Mount Desert Island in the summer."

Tim made a noise that was meant to be "No" but came out more like "Nmph" as he swallowed the last corner of his greasy sandwich and licked off his fingers. "I mean a proper island, with the sea all round, and cliffs and beaches. Back home I go for rambles on Walney Island to clear my head."

"I don't want a clear head! Hard enough to drown your sorrows in this country, with the pubs all closing at eleven."

"I reckon we just learn to drink faster." Tim folded his arms on the table, crumbs clinging to his Christmas jumper. "How late do the pubs in New York stay open, then?"

"Four a.m. if you're still standing. We don't even start going out until things here would be shutting down."

Tim made goalposts with the thumb and forefinger of one hand and flicked a large crumb through. "You could try sending her a telegram."

"Do they still exist?"

"Dunno—you read about them in books."

"Yeah, there are lotsa things you read about in books that don't exist." Malcolm hauled himself up to make coffee, but his jar of instant was empty.

Towards the end of Hilary Term Professor Barraclough sent him to see the Royal Shakespeare Company's *Midsummer Night's Dream* at the Barbican. Malcolm had been there before, but still got lost in the bleak gray maze of concert halls, art galleries, apartment complexes, and cinemas bounded by the ancient London city wall. He missed curtain-up and slipped in on Lysander declaring: "One turf shall serve as pillow for us both; One heart, one bed, two bosoms, and one troth... Then by your side no bed-room me deny, For, lying so, Hermia, I do not lie... "

He barely made the last train back to Oxford from Paddington; what kind of city would have a subway system that stopped running at half past midnight? Or shut down Tube stops near the theatre district even earlier? From the West End it was always touch and go. As he fell into bed he spotted black mold growing on his bedspread in a speckled spray fanned out around the base of the naked water pipe running up the wall, beaded with condensation. Even without mold, it was the ugliest duvet he'd ever seen—mottled green spackled with circles and triangles of dusty beige and salmon pink—but when he flipped it over, the reverse was worse: sullen slate blue pocked with the same capricious pink and tan geometry. It surprised him how much he hated it; then again, the room was so small, there wasn't much else to look at.

His feet hung over the edge of the bed that was inexplicably short for a country with a tall population—yet the duvet was even shorter, almost square, barely spanning ankles to shoulders, slipping off sideways when he rolled over—none of which mattered when Emma stayed over. She would have done a better job with Helena—made her angrier and funnier, less hysterical, less pathetic. He lay scrunched up uncomfortably, wanting her even as he told himself it was pointless to want someone on a different continent when there were 30,000 students, half of them female, right here in the same city—and went on wanting her, a foreign feeling. Was she giving him the push, as they said here? He was used to being the pusher, not the pushee; the possibility hadn't crossed his mind till Tim raised it.

Halfway through high school he'd grown into his facial features and gone from being a quiet kid nobody noticed, to one most girls—and a few boys—pursued. This confused him till he grasped its convenience: getting girls took little effort on his part. But the physical forces at work could not obscure the fact that two people flung together for no better reason did not have much to say to each other before, during, or after. At least when all else failed, Brits talked about the weather; in America, the conversational crutch was TV: teenagers took watching the same shows as proof of deep kinship. But Malcolm didn't watch TV; when he was at loose ends, he read a book. Which left him with two choices: say so and ruin his chances, or nod a lot and try not to glance at his watch. But with Emma his impulse was to chuck it out the window, and time with it.

Running across the quad to his tutorial—lately he was running late for everything—the great bell tolling over the gate rebuked his tardiness with the authority of centuries. Was this how MPs felt, late for sessions of Parliament, as Big Ben boomed out over Westminster? Somehow the bigger the bell, the graver the offense: you couldn't blame a defective wristwatch when the whole city could hear the clock strike.

Professor Barraclough, working at his desk, waved Malcolm to a chair and went on writing as Malcolm began, out of breath, to read his essay on *A Midsummer Night's Dream*: "Helena sets the tone of the play inversely by observing that 'Things base and vile, holding no quantity, / Love can transpose to form and dignity,' when in fact the opposite occurs, as when Demetrius remarks, 'my love to Hermia, / Melted as the snow, seems to me now / As the remembrance of an idle gawd / Which in my childhood I did dote upon.' One wonders what difference it makes who ends up with whom, when even the 'right' pairings make each other miserable, as, for example, when Hermia says of Lysander, 'O! then, what graces in my love do dwell, / That she hath turned a heaven unto a hell—'"

Professor Barraclough cleared his throat. "I believe that's '*he* hath turned,' isn't it?"

"Right—sorry." Malcolm read on: "... When Helena begs her true love Demetrius to 'Use me but as your spaniel, spurn me... Neglect me, lose me; only give me leave... to follow you' and he replies 'I am sick when I do look on thee... I'll run from thee and hide me in the brakes, / And leave thee to the mercy of wild beasts,' one can only agree with Helena that 'Nor hath Love's mind of any judgment taste... And therefore is Love said to be a child, / Because he is in choice so oft beguil'd—'"

Professor Barraclough cleared his throat again. "You do realize, don't you, that this is a comedy?"

I used to, Malcolm thought. Aloud he said, "Maybe it was the leather costumes, but this production came across more like black comedy. Theseus's 'Lovers and madmen have such seething brains' speech seemed to strike the truer note of love's ultimate nihilism, whereas Oberon's final upbeat benediction felt tacked on according to convention."

"Yes. Well." Professor Barraclough leaned

back in his chair and extracted two navy blue volumes of the *Oxford English Dictionary* from a wall of bookshelves tilted slightly inward, like the top-heavy houses in medieval streets. "I must caution you against using the terms 'nihilism' and 'upbeat' anachronistically in conjunction with Shakespeare." He licked his thumb to turn the pages. "'Nihilism' did not enter the English language until 1817, and 'upbeat' not till 1947. So Shakespeare could hardly have had either in mind as a guiding principle of composition."

At the end of the hour, Professor Barraclough asked abruptly, "You've not gone and fallen unhappily in love too, have you? When a young man goes from effervescent to putrescent in a matter of weeks, I've found that's often the case." He closed his copy of *A Midsummer Night's Dream.* "You'd do well to keep in mind you can do that at home. You ought to devote all your energies to taking full advantage of Oxford. If you squander your time here, you'll regret it." He slid the two volumes of the *OED* back into place. "You mustn't let love get in the way of literature—or at least wait till we do the tragedies."

After attending an Oxford Union debate with the proposition "This House Believes American Culture Is an Oxymoron," Malcolm ignored this sort of English snobbery as a matter of course. The brick walls of the Union's garden had been plastered with the bright red posters stuck up all over town since the start of term: the rear view of a man flashing his trenchcoat at a nude female statue, with the caption: EXPOSE YOURSELF TO THE OXFORD UNION. The debate proved to be as entertaining as it was patronizing, but Malcolm still walked out the "Noes" door afterwards. He could never bring himself to point out that the heirs to such a vastly superior culture ought to be above America-bashing, because he too had bought into the myth of British excellence—why else would he be here?

So he didn't answer, just shifted uncomfortably in the low chair, because his clothes, which had hung loosely, now fit snugly after two months of heavy drinking and inactivity, so that he was unpleasantly aware of them. At least, he thought, I've taken full advantage of Oxford's pubs.

Saturday morning he dragged himself out of bed and down to the Post Office before it closed at noon-thirty, slipping inside the main branch in St. Aldate's just as they locked the outer gate against latecomers. Mothering Sunday, as it was called in the UK, had snuck up on him, and he had vindictive reasons for making sure whatever he sent his mother arrived early. He felt dizzy and winded from cycling so fast and furiously first thing after the shock of getting vertical; the pile of stamps they slid out to him under the ticket window swam before his eyes. "You'd think this was some kind of backwards, Third World nation."

He paused between lickings as the taste of the adhesive threatened to turn his stomach. "Why the hell don't they have postage meters? I've got enough stamps here to mail myself home!"

When he'd finished, it was well past opening time, the Bulldog three doors up, the Old Tom right next door. Pubs were reassuring in a way bars couldn't be: not deliberately old-fashioned, just plain old. Sitting in them felt as if nothing had ever changed and never would. Like refrigeration: he'd always counted on the coldness of American beer to blunt its taste, but the warm beer in England was less unsettling to a shaky stomach.

Walking his bike home a few pints later, too rocky to ride it, the pace of pedestrians and timing of traffic lights galled him. In New York everyone but tourists kept to a brisk canter, and as long as DON'T WALK flashed, there was still time to cross the street. But Oxford was as thick with tourists as Times Square—something he would not have thought possible—and the locals didn't move much faster. He was forever getting stalled out behind them, yet had to gallop to make it through pelican crossings before the green man stopped beeping.

He was a block from home before it dawned on him that it was now mid-March and American Mother's Day was not till May.

He didn't even ride all the way back to the flat after his last tutorial of Hilary Term, but left his bike locked at Gloucester Green—knowing full well it would not be there when he returned—and hopped on the blue-and-yellow Oxford CityLink express to Heathrow without bothering to pack a bag. As the coach lumbered down the High, Magdalen's gargoyles were at eye level; they were not all monsters as he'd assumed from below: lions and monkeys, lovers embracing flashed past his window.

For the first time in his life, he'd neglected to bring a book to read and, without one, paced the departure lounge waiting for boarding call. In desperation, he bought a Baedeker's *British Isles* from WHSmith, but the glossy, full-color pages bore little resemblance to the quaint turns of phrase cited by credulous tourists in E. M. Forster novels. He read as far as the Outer Hebrides before he fell asleep somewhere over the North Atlantic.

Easter Vacs 1991

Malcolm's legs were so cramped after the plane and shuttle bus from JFK to Grand Central, he skipped the subway and walked down Park Avenue, outpacing the gridlock, timing his stride to hit the green lights at each block. Every other car was yellow, and horns echoed down the tunnel of tall buildings, overlapped and redoubled. He'd never thought of New York as clean, but after Oxford's soot-black sandstone, Midtown's glass skyscrapers gleamed. Scents shifted and re-settled: burnt pretzels, the tang of mustard and sauerkraut supplanted stomach-turning kebab grease. He didn't even like hot dogs, but their smell was no less comforting for that. He had to fight his way against the tide rushing toward Grand Central, but felt at home crushed in the crowd: this was how cities were supposed to be.

Fourth Avenue's anomalous existence for six

blocks downtown always felt like an oversight, but for the most part streets in the East Village—unlike streets in London—were numbered and ran perpendicular, so it was easy to find the address. Rusty fire escapes that did not look safe to stand on ran across the windows of the building's upper floors; otherwise it was an unremarkable brick walk-up. He pressed the buzzer, wondering if it worked; this looked like the kind of building where the odds were not so good.

"Yes? Who is it?" Emma's voice said through the intercom.

"Malcolm."

There was no answer but the static hiss. "Hey, are you there?" he started to say, but then the buzzer sounded and he climbed five flights up to her floor.

"What are you doing here?" She didn't take the chain off.

"Can I come in?"

"Just a moment. Jenny!" she called over her shoulder. "Are you decent?"

"How decent do you need?" a high-pitched, slightly husky American voice called back.

"It seems we have a gentleman caller," Emma drawled in a lazy parody of Tennessee Williams.

"Oh! OK, half a sec."

Some scuffling and bumping, then he was let in.

"Hi! Bye!" said a fair-skinned girl with dimples and long corkscrew curls of ash-blond hair falling forward over her shoulders. "I'll be back in a few—I mean, no, I won't—I've got tons of errands to do!" She pulled the door shut behind her.

The room was painted the color of acorn squash innards and split in two by means of Chinese screens. Malcolm had never understood how anyone—let alone two people—could squeeze into a studio, but now, compared to his room in Oxford, even half of this seemed spacious. Emma, barefoot, was wearing an enormous old sweatshirt with the neck and cuffs cut out.

"What's the big idea?" he asked her.

"Of my stopping in New York?" She raised her eyebrows. "It was the chance of a lifetime. I hope you didn't think I'd pass it up on your account."

"I'm not that much of a Neanderthal! I mean, what's the big idea not returning my calls or answering my letters?"

Her eyebrows subsided. "When you're always banging on about how you hate telephones? Wasn't that your excuse for turning up backstage unannounced? You couldn't manage to talk and count change at the same time?"

"We've only got a payphone in the flat. I had to go to the train station to call you on a card phone."

"Is that what all the din was in the background? I could scarcely catch a word you said. You come across much better in person." She flung him a smile.

"Didn't you get my letters?"

She assumed an attitude of mock dismay. "I

simply can't keep pace with the current onslaught of fan mail."

"*Through the Wringer* closed." He was now armed with a copy of the latest *New Yorker*, rolled up in the pocket of his raincoat—the only coat he ever wore in England. "Are you planning to stay here indefinitely, or go back to London?"

"I'll stay on for a bit and see what comes along—I've a good waitressing job."

"Where?"

"Unter den Linden, near Gramercy—"

"Yeah, I know it. People tip well there, especially in June—scent of the linden trees goes to their heads. Stroke of genius to put in that rooftop biergarten." She didn't seem too pleased to see him, so he didn't dare stop talking, lest she ask him to leave. "Are you in line for any more acting jobs?"

"Time will tell. I've got a reading for *Sweeney Agonistes*."

"That's only ten pages long! It's not even finished."

"Well, someone has finished it now. Someone other than Eliot, I mean. By interpolating bits of the other Sweeney poems."

"Sounds god-awful."

"A reading's a reading." She gave his sleeve a tug. "You can take off that mack any time, love. There's no London fog in here."

He unzipped it, but felt stiff and sluggish in mind, body, and soul. He couldn't follow

Emma's fickle body language or work out how it corresponded to her speech. "Even after *Through the Wringer* closed, you couldn't find time to write once?" He'd spent so many hours rattling back and forth on trains to London to see her—though to be fair, he'd slogged through lots of readings and essays en route.

"I did tell you I'd gone, didn't I? What more did you expect? Long-distance love affairs aren't a sound investment of time." She turned away to tidy up the piles of clothing strewn about the floor.

Malcolm didn't answer. What could he say to this woman who had dominated—not to say oppressed—his thoughts for all of Hilary Term without giving him a second thought, who spoke of love affairs the way his father dispensed stock tips?

"Your letters sounded so dull and gloomy." She picked up a tea towel with faded fruits printed on it. "In London you were much more lively."

Malcolm couldn't figure out why none of these cutting remarks were cutting him to the quick; he was too dizzy with not touching her. "I didn't come all this way to argue."

"Could've fooled me." She shook out the towel so hard it made a snapping sound. "What did you come for? Tea and crumpets?"

"Yeah, I've been so starved for those in England."

She laughed. "Tea and strumpets?" And gave him the sideways look that unraveled whatever held him together.

"You're getting warmer."

Emma dropped the tea towel where she'd found it. "Clearly that's what Jenny had in mind when she bolted." She held out her arms for his coat and hung it on one corner of the Chinese screen. "Blimey, you smell like England!"

"How do you mean?" To him England smelled like beer brewing and coal burning.

"Dunno . . . different laundry detergent?" She let her hair down from the topknot out of which it had been splayed in all directions. "Shall we put up our swords, then?"

"About time." He seized her sword arm and drew her close enough to kiss; they stood pressed together on the one clear patch of floor in the room's center.

"Can't do this long-distance, can you?"

Malcolm, whose lips were otherwise engaged, did not reply—fringe benefit of foreplay: there were so many other things to do with your mouth besides talk.

"You've finally taken to drinking beer, haven't you?" she observed, helping him off with his sweater.

"'I learn'd it in England, where, indeed, they are most potent in potting.'" He slid down her sweatpants. "But I still don't like it."

She tugged at his shirt-tails, unbuttoning. "Why drink it, then?"

He thought, "Because 'Ale's the stuff to drink For fellows whom it hurts to think.'" But said, "What else is there in that blasted country of yours?"

"Gin, of course."

"In February?"

"Cider, then. You used to drink that, didn't you?"

But Malcolm by now had his mind and his hands on other things. Emma smelled faintly of oranges, and there wasn't anything more alive. Some foresighted passengers on the flight over had packed a picnic, and when they got to dessert, unleashed droplets of orange essence—sunshine in a skin—enlivened the stale air of the whole 747.

"Oh dear, that's lovely, isn't it? Shove those scripts off my bed, won't you, love? I'd better close the blinds."

They plunged into each other, and by the time they were sprawled out, spent, Malcolm didn't think he could move, even if he'd wanted to; he was pins and needles all over, head spinning. "I flew three thousand miles to see you and you weren't going to let me in at first—I know you weren't."

Emma didn't contradict him. "Did you really?" She sat up and stared down at him. "Bloody expensive way to get your kicks."

"I bought a student ticket."

"Still bloody expensive—but it makes good advertising." She reached for her sweatshirt. "Not every girl can brag a bloke flew five thousand kilometers to boff her!"

Malcolm yawned and stretched. "I don't know

that I'd do it again." He wasn't sure if he was trying to be offensive or not. Everything about him felt leaden and lazy, even his tongue. His eyes drooped shut.

Emma kept silent getting dressed, then clapped her hands. "All right, end of the pity party! Up off the bed—I've got lines to learn!" And threw his clothes in his face.

"I thought it was a read-through. Why do you have to learn them?" He didn't feel like getting dressed yet. He liked lying in Emma's bed, where he could still smell her on the sheets.

"Because I can focus more on how to say them if I'm not stumbling over them. I can't do both straight off when I've also got to see to my face and body language. They expect that, you know."

"Want me to read the other parts for you?" he offered, afraid otherwise he'd have to leave.

She stopped picking up the pages of her script. "On one condition."

"What's that?" He sat up and felt strangely disoriented, unsure which articles of clothing went on first.

"Promise not to read them well. Just prompt me."

"Why?" He stood up to put on his jeans.

"It's too distracting whilst I'm still learning—I might start ad libbing in response."

"That I'd like to see!" He sat back down without tucking in his shirt; all that beer made his jeans hard to button.

"I may be able to earn a few extra quid as a dialect coach." Emma seated herself so close to him he could feel her body heat. "The American actors I've met say those tapes you buy to practice with are worse than useless. The examples are about as likely as '*J'ai la plume de ma tante*,' apparently. But I could pronounce for them what they'll actually be saying, and in my opinion it would be money well spent. Most of them sound ghastly doing Shakespeare—or even Oscar Wilde."

"Probably about as ghastly as the average British attempt at an American accent." He leaned in closer and caught the faint scent of oranges again. "Why do Brits always do Midwestern? That's as foreign to me as Britspeak—sounds like all the American characters are meant to be dim-witted politicians."

"Well, aren't they?"

"Ha ha."

"No need to get hot under the collar, love." She smoothed his hair out of his eyes. "Your British accent's excellent."

"Probably because I'm not an actor." He flopped back among the pillows. "I've had to use it in real life to get decent service."

Malcolm didn't keep his promise to read badly. When they reached the part where Sweeney tries to lure Doris off to a tropical island, he couldn't resist adjusting Sweeney's lines to suit his own purposes—with better results than Sweeney achieved, since Emma did end up ad libbing with him.

"You're really good, you know," he told her as they were getting dressed for the second time that evening. "All last term, I didn't see anyone else as good on stage."

Emma paused, one leg in, one leg out of her sweatpants. "Aren't you meant to use that line before you get me in the sack?"

"I wanted you to believe it."

"Not likely—you were going to the RSC!"

"There's always room for improvement."

"Not at this rate! I ask you not to get too involved reading the play, so instead you decide to live it. I'll never learn my lines this way."

"Maybe we should skip ahead to a different section. All that birth and death and copulation's hard to ignore when I'm sitting next to you."

"Likewise, I'm sure." She fastened her hair back up on top of her head. "Perhaps you'd better sit elsewhere, if you can't read any worse than that."

"Not necessary. I'm sure I'll do a crap job as the other whore. What's her name again?"

"Dusty. All the same, I think I'll stand. You remember things better in the same position you learn them in."

This time through, she angled herself away from him to project all her emotions and gestures at a framed black-and-white photo of the Flatiron Building; this felt to Malcolm like watching a show from a partial-view seat.

Just as jet lag was catching up with him, a key turned in the lock and Jenny let herself in. "Reading scripts together already?" She dumped her grocery bags on the stove; there was no counter. "You'll have to introduce us now, Emma, whether you like it or not."

"Genevieve Doucette, Malcolm Forrester. He just popped over from London to say hello. He's not an actor."

"Why not? He looks like one. No fair for you to have English hotties chasing after you too!"

"Actually, I'm from New York." Malcolm stood to shake hands. "I live uptown." With this familiar phrase he felt more like himself; when he said he lived in Osney Town, only Chaucer scholars knew where he meant.

"For how long?" Emma asked.

"I don't know. I've got six weeks of vacs."

"And once they're over, you'll go back?"

"I guess so—I don't know." The edge in her voice was making him feel gelatinous again.

Jenny looked from one to the other of them, unsure whether to smile or frown. She fiddled with her jewelry and adjusted the safety clasp on her watch. "Didn't you have to work tonight?" she asked Emma. "I thought you'd be long gone by now."

"Bloody hell!" Emma dropped her script. "Would you excuse us, please?" She grabbed Malcolm by the arm and dragged him out into the hallway. "You've got to leave," she told him.

"And please don't come back."

"What are you talking about? Why not?"

"I can't afford to keep losing track of time with you like this."

"Isn't that good? It is for me." From inside, he could hear Jenny singing some song about blackbirds.

"Not if I lose my job, it's not." Emma shut the door behind her.

Malcolm stared at her, confused. The only job he'd ever had was teaching tennis at a country club on Long Island, and getting there on time hadn't been an issue, since his grandmother, with whom he'd spent the summer, lived down the street. "They're not going to fire you just for missing one shift, are they?" His father had remained a workaholic even after his mother was no longer around to avoid, but kids his own age were forever switching their schedules last-minute or calling in sick so they could go to afternoon baseball games or wait on line for concert tickets.

"I guess I'll find out, won't I?" Emma folded her arms across her chest.

"Even if they do, it's not like there's a restaurant shortage in New York."

"I don't want to work in some dive!" Her voice rose. "I make good tips where I am now."

"Yeah, but you could do better uptown—"

"For your information, it's not only the filthy rich who know how to tip. Ordinary people appreciate being treated like human beings for a change."

"I'm sure they do, but that doesn't help you unless they can afford to appreciate it consistently."

"Don't be such an arrogant prick!"

"I'm not being an arrogant prick." His home turf accent was seeping back into his voice, and with it words into his head—words much worse than hers. They were easy; they were what he knew best. But he didn't want to go where they would lead him. "I thought we were talking about restaurants."

"We are."

"All I'm saying is, if tips are your main concern, you could do better than Unter den Linden."

"Yes, but then I'd have to learn who all the rich and famous clientele are, and pretend I cared." She made a face.

"So what's the problem? Pretending's what you do best."

"That's not the point! They don't even necessarily tip better, the cheap bastards—"

"No, but some of them might back plays." His mother had among her lovers, at last count, a real-estate developer who dabbled in producing and was forever moaning about money down the toilet, yet had an endless supply to flush after it. But Emma was staring at him like he'd fallen from space, so he figured his family was better forgotten; no one really liked those inconclusive stories prized by *The New Yorker*, where nobody ever won so it all seemed as insignificant and depressing as reality. Why telling this kind of story made you a great writer in literary circles—when in real life it made you a great bore—was a mystery.

"They might," she said, "or they might not. Gramercy's convenient. I don't want to commute all the way to the Upper East Side."

"Not that far up! People just live there—they're not quarantined."

"Well, you should know."

"What the hell is that supposed to mean?" His stomach was starting to feel the way it did when he was little and his parents stumbled home late shouting at each other and woke him up.

"It means it's easy for you to tell me not to worry. I can't risk changing jobs when I've not got a green card—what am I supposed to live on whilst I'm unemployed? Not all of us are lucky enough to be so flush with cash."

"Not all of us are so full of shit either."

"I beg your pardon?" Her eyes narrowed at him.

"New York's no more expensive than London, the exchange rate's two to one in your favor, and the tips at Unter den Linden are more than you could hope for from any pub. People hardly tip at all in England—you taught me that yourself. You can only be better off here than you were over there."

Emma bit her lip. "True, but that does me no good if they fire me and I get deported."

Malcolm lost patience. "What kind of actress are you, if you can't talk your way out of one minor infraction?"

"Bloody wanker!" Emma glared at him. "I'd best be off to talk my way out of it—and you'd best be gone!" She fairly leaped back inside her apartment, threw his coat out at him, and slammed the door.

Malcolm suddenly needed to sit down, but there were no chairs. He'd suspected his impromptu visit might be a bad idea, but not that it had the potential to be this bad. He didn't know what had gone wrong, but he knew there was no reasoning with a slammed door. On the street his feet moved forward of their own accord, taking him towards Second, past the Thirsty Scholar—no, not past. Long and narrow, dark and crowded—he slid inside, knew no one, and saw he hadn't timed his trip well: Oxford's three terms did not match up with American semesters, so none of his friends would be home for spring break. This too was disturbing: he never lost his head over girls to the point of poor planning, yet could think of nothing else to do till it was late enough to sneak into his mother's apartment unnoticed. He'd lost track of who she was married to at the moment, and didn't want to deal with introductions.

At least in the time remaining he could drink enough to fall asleep in short order, if he paced himself: there was nothing worse than tanking up too quickly, only to wake at 3 a.m. dehydrated and sober. He ordered straight shots of bourbon, relieved he wouldn't have to work his way through six or seven imperial pints of whatever was on tap in hopes of learning to like it. At least at American frat parties everyone expected the keg contents to taste like bat piss; no one pretended they emptied it for any reason other than to get wasted.

After three or four rounds he noticed a girl with short magenta hair—possibly meant to be red—advancing down the bar towards him, one stool at a time. She wore the boxy black eyeglasses favored by art students and a lime-green halter top with complicated straps. When she gained possession of the stool next to his, she plunked her drink down and pushed the glasses up on top of her head, so that her eyes suddenly shrank. "You can't be as desperate as you look—not when you look like that."

"Desperate enough to get airsick."

"I know a cure for desperation." She slid her glass against his. "Bet you do too."

"On the contrary," he said, still feeling foreign and British, "I've already seen to that."

"Then what the hell are you doing here?" she laughed, not buying this. "You're supposed to hit the bars before, not after!" She looked down at their empties; her roots were black.

"Couldn't wait that long." He settled both their tabs with a pile of crumpled fives and tens as a disincentive to further intercourse. At some point he'd noticed that if you pulled crisp, large bills out of a leather wallet, people assumed there were plenty more to follow; whereas if you dug dilapidated smaller specimens out of the depths of various pockets, they figured you were draining the dregs and lost interest. In England he'd liked the novelty of sliding pound coins across the bar, but most Americans he ran into were appalled that a mere coin could be worth two whole dollars, yet slip through their fingers quickly as a quarter.

Magenta Hair moved on in search of brighter prospects, leaving him to his bourbon. All around, throaty American voices slurred an antidote to precise British intonations. When the fire brigade roared by, drowning out the last ten seconds of the Rangers game with deafening slider sirens—not those feeble European out-of-tune doorbells—it sounded to his ears like a benediction.

"Malcolm!" Someone—his father—was shaking him by the shoulder. "What are you doing here?"

"Not sleeping, that's for sure." He tried to roll away from the intrusion.

His father kicked the bedstead, hard. "What are you doing here? I haven't got all day, even if you do."

"Bloody hell!" He pried his eyes open. "Must've given the driver the wrong address—meant to go to Mother's." Who did not arise early enough herself to interfere with other people's hangovers.

"I mean, what are you doing in this country? Aren't you supposed to be in England all year—or have you gotten expelled and deported?"

Thanks for the vote of confidence, thought

Malcolm. "Relax, Pop. It's the vacs."

"What?"

"Term ended yesterday," he explained in an accent somewhere between BBC and Oxbridge. "I'm on holiday, vacation, R & R—"

"It's not like you to come home for vacations. I thought you might've gotten kicked out."

"Interesting theory, Pop," Malcolm said into the pillow. "Only it's not like me to get kicked out either, is it?"

"Not lately, no. Weren't you planning to travel over spring break?"

"Flying three thousand miles isn't traveling?" He switched back to New Yorkese for simplicity's sake.

"In Europe, by train. You hate flying."

"Who doesn't?" He pulled the pillow over his eyes. "Shouldn't you be heading downtown soon? You said you didn't have all day to interrogate me."

"Lucky for you, I don't." His father left the room without further comment.

When Malcolm resurfaced several hours later, it occurred to him that the apartment mix-up was for the best; his mother was not to be so easily put off by the necessity of going to work, since her hours as a fit model were irregular at best. He lay still, relishing the over-zealous American central heating that had freed him, for the first time in months, to sleep in boxer shorts and

T-shirt instead of flannel pajamas, flannel sheets, and thick socks whenever Emma wasn't there to help warm up the bed. But he would rather have slept in a cold room with her than a warm room without her.

He had second thoughts about coming home at all when he met his eyes, barely more than slits, in the bathroom mirror and saw his skiing tan had faded to a sickly pallor not unlike the albino Wensleydale cheese that so alarmed him in British supermarkets, alarming in themselves: you had to pay a deposit for shopping carts (which they called trolleys), and grocery bags (which they called carrier bags) cost extra. But he shrugged this off; parents had to learn sooner or later that their children were old enough to behave as badly as adults.

He took an obscenely long shower, making the most of the powerful hot water pipes in his father's building while he had the chance. Even the coin-operated showers in youth hostels on the Continent were less feeble than the ancient English dribbles that passed for plumbing in Oxford. Hands down, America's great contribution to world culture was sound plumbing.

As the clouds of steam displaced the fog of sleep, he took stock of the situation. Normally he would have been happy to get laid twice in one evening and leave it at that; there'd been occasions when getting kicked out afterwards would have been a reprieve. But in this case he would have been happy—almost—to read scripts all night and leave it at that. Drying off, a headache seemed preferable to heartache, so he abstained from aspirin.

He didn't bother to investigate the kitchen before venturing out; his father was the kind of housekeeper whose refrigerator seldom held more than a jar of olives, a lime, a lemon, tonic water, and—if you were lucky—cream; the freezer, ice cubes, gin, and coffee. He bought a half-gallon carton of Tropicana and a giant can of tomato juice at the nearest deli, holding up the line at the register as he fumbled with bills all the same size and color and coins shrunk small and unfamiliar.

He detoured through the park, treading on the dead grass in long-distance defiance of Oxford's pristine squares of green roped off like sacred relics. Then nearly got flattened by a bus barreling down the right side of the road low-slung and incognito after London's big red double-deckers. He leapt back onto the curb like an out-of-towner, reflexes too scrambled by left-hand drive to jaywalk, waiting for the red light to turn yellow on its way to green, as they did in England.

Once he'd put his juice in the fridge to chill, he was at a loss; his itinerary had not included a Plan B. But he knew better than to make contact first thing in the morning after a disaster, even if only one of the parties in question was hung-over. No matter how many times he overdid it, the next morning's retribution still surprised him; instead of huddling under the covers, he roamed aimlessly, waiting with unwarranted patience for his misery to subside, as if it were something he could walk off like a twisted ankle or a stitch in the side.

He checked to see if anything had changed in his absence, but nothing had. Nothing ever did, except those cleaning ladies unfortunate enough to lack a photographic sense of spatial relationship. If Malcolm's father couldn't find things post-dusting, he found someone else to dust.

When Malcolm's mother, years earlier, had conveyed to him her intention to depart, Malcolm pretended to be hurt but was in fact mainly bewildered as to why she hadn't done so long before. Most of his friends' parents were divorced; it seemed anomalous to him that his were not, when they so clearly ought to be. She left in the middle of the afternoon, while his father was at work; Malcolm suspected she'd intended to be gone before he himself got home from school, but was running late in this as in all else. Caught in the act, she started sentences she couldn't finish: "Your father... We can't... I need..."

When he tired of watching her squirm under his silence, Malcolm asked what she planned to take with her.

"As if! I've been trying to get your father to redecorate for more years than I care to remember. You'll be stuck with all this till he kicks the bucket."

Though the antiques that had oppressed his mother were easy on the eye—claw-footed sofas and wing chairs, glazed porcelain lamps, graceful tables with curved hips and slender ankles, inlaid with mother-of-pearl or topped with marble—Malcolm only cared about the books: two sets of floor-to-ceiling shelves behind glass doors with keys left in the locks, poetry on the left, prose on the right, alphabetized by author, ancient crumbly hardcovers inscribed with old-fashioned names like Silas and Ida, nineteenth-century dates, and out-of-the-way places in Massachusetts.

"Who are all these people?" he once asked his father, who replied without interest: "Ancestors. I can't keep the names straight. They've been handed down forever and ever, Amen."

"But Massachusetts!" Malcolm protested—too late, for his father had already gone off under the assumption that the conversation had ended.

Until he went to boarding school, everyone Malcolm knew lived in the tri-state area. Massachusetts was a place you read about in history books, where grim-looking Pilgrims wearing witch hats with the points lopped off declined to decorate their churches, reserving their inventiveness to lynch witches masquerading as old women. Massachusetts was the state you most needed to speed through on the way to Bar Harbor, since there were no restrooms at the so-called rest stops on I-495. Harvard was there, and Boston—but no one in New York bothered much about Boston.

Before he was old enough to know better, Malcolm thought every book in the world was enshrined in those two towering cases, so authoritative was their organization. In fact most of the literary canon was, making book reports a breeze but causing confusion in conversation: when he said, "Let's sit in the library," people thought he meant the New York Public, not a room in his own apartment.

Older, it dawned on him that not all families had the same priorities. Other people's living rooms had massive walls of shelves, but often they held stereos or plants or knick-knacks or large-screen TVs. If there were books, they were as likely to be arranged by size or color as by content, if arranged at all. Sometimes there were garish rows of hardcover bestsellers, all by the same author, in mint condition, as if no one had ever read them; sometimes there were no books at all, just glossy magazines artfully scattered.

This type of apartment felt unreal to Malcolm, like a furniture display in a department store or a stage where the set dresser ran out of budget or inspiration. Spending time in them made him uneasy, as if he'd landed in a foreign country with no luggage. What did these people do with themselves, he wondered. What would he do when he got bored? He never watched TV; his parents' habit of throwing china at each other had left him with an aversion to the sudden, loud noises of television, so it dismayed him to find in most households the set got flicked on—and left on—as automatically as the lights or heat.

He stumbled on a stratagem when his mother dragged him as a decoy to a friend's son's confirmation party in one of the sleek apartments with no books. His mother had designs on this friend's husband; Malcolm didn't really know the kid in question, had no desire to get better acquainted, and was considering the fire stairs, when he noticed the one friend of his parents he liked—mostly because she never tried to talk to him—was also there. She was a highly successful lawyer married to another highly successful lawyer living in childless splendor on Central Park West in a building favored by reclusive rock stars for its private elevators. Malcolm had never seen this woman do anything other than read, no matter what kind of party she was at, or who was there. His mother said she was stuck-up, his father that she was shy; Malcolm thought they were both wrong and that she just had better things to do and did them. She spoke so seldom Malcolm wasn't sure he'd recognize her voice, though she'd been to their apartment dozens of times, always gravitating to the library, where she selected a book and settled down in a wing chair to be happily overlooked until her husband decided it was time to leave.

This behavior made perfect sense to Malcolm, so he trailed her at a distance, wondering what she'd do when she found the bookshelves were bare. At length she chose a chair as comfy as chairs got in this kind of apartment, crossed her legs, and pulled a thick paperback out of her Gucci pocketbook. As soon as he got home, Malcolm experimented: he could just cram a volume of Everyman's Library or The Modern Library into the pocket of his prep school blazer. His mother was pleased to find him dressing the part without the usual threats and coercion, until she figured out why. "At least if you read your hosts' books, it looks like you think they have good taste in literature. Bringing your own's like showing up at a New Year's Eve party with a private bottle of champagne—and it ruins the drape of your jacket."

"If they had good taste, I wouldn't need to bring my own!" Malcolm pointed out, to no avail.

Now he stared at the gilt titles reflected in the glass doors, wondering what would take his mind off Emma till enough time had elapsed for her to have cooled down. So many choices made his head spin when he was hung-over; he closed his eyes and pointed: *The Complete Poetical Works of Spenser*. Not exactly a page-turner, but he remembered being the only person in English 101 to like the excerpts from *The Faerie Queene*; might as well read more of that.

He found a cut-glass pitcher in the butler's pantry, filled it with orange juice and ice cubes, and took it into the library with a rocks glass. It felt luxurious to have unlimited ice: their freezer in Oxford—a small shelf in the top of the fridge—produced nothing but snow; occasionally they excavated and found some desiccated peas or a lost lump of cheese. He flopped down on one of the window seats and opened to the editor's introduction: "When the first three books of the *Faerie Queen* were published in 1590, Spenser had been at work upon the poem for at least ten years..." He skipped over the seventeen dedicatory sonnets and began Book I, Canto I.

When the phone rang half a dozen cantos later, he almost answered it—then didn't, in case it was his mother, who made a point of calling his father whenever she had news likely to upset him. After it stopped ringing, it occurred to him that she knew her ex-husband wouldn't be home at this hour on a weekday and was unlikely to squander her spite on a mere recording. Could Emma have figured out his phone number? She seemed somehow to have gleaned his neighborhood. Did he look like he lived on the Upper East Side? The thought was depressing.

He dialed in to retrieve the message, but the access code had been changed since his last visit, so he called his father's secretary, who was paid to be omniscient.

"Back from England already?" Martha's slight Southern drawl was complicated by adenoids.

"Sort of."

"Do you like it over there?"

"Sort of."

"That much?" she laughed. "Or did you stay out too late last night?"

"Exactly," Malcolm said. "That's why I need to know who called."

"Oh, one of *those* nights." Martha weighted the word with several extra syllables. "B-E-A-R."

"Why? Is the market about to crash?"

"More than it's done already with a war on? I don't think so, hon, but it's been a rough week."

"Thanks for the warning."

He dialed in again and heard the voice of Dolores Gottlieb, a friend of his mother's, addressing his father in intimate terms. Her son Nathan was in England for the year, and thus far Malcolm had succeeded in avoiding him on all but one or two occasions. He saved the message and judged it safe by now to head downtown to see Emma. He left Spenser on the window seat and put the orange juice back in the fridge.

The day had deteriorated since his trip to the store, so he threw on his raincoat and ran for the subway. One of the things he'd missed most in England was subway tokens. To a New Yorker, it made no sense that you needed a ticket to leave the Underground as well as to enter it, and he was forever rifling his pockets at the exits to Tube stations, having forgotten this. The Tube cars seemed strange too, with their upholstered seats—like a living room that went shooting sideways—their rubber tires creepily quiet. Now the shriek of steel wheels split his skull and the boxy cars seemed spacious after the curved sides of the Tube, where he could only stand up straight in the center. MTA drivers slurred through "Pleestancleeruhdaclosindaws" in less time than it took the pre-recorded male voice on the Tube to warn riders to "Mind the gap!" Malcolm kept expecting this foreign tagline to follow the unintelligible New York stop announcements—which in London were delivered by a recorded female voice as refined as her male counterpart, and mildly tranquilized.

For this kind of weather I could've stayed in England, he thought, trudging to Emma's building through a fine but persistent drizzle.

"What do you want?" Through the speaker her voice sounded harsh and metallic.

"To talk to you. What do you think?"

"I'm sorry, but I haven't time."

"Why not?"

"I'm due at work soon."

"I thought you kicked me out because I'd lost you that job."

"As it happens, I've talked my way back into it."

"Then what are you still mad at me for?"

There was no answer.

"Emma? Don't make me stand here talking to a bunch of holes in your lobby wall. Lemme in, willya? I won't stay long."

The buzzer sounded, and when he'd legged the five flights up to her floor, he found her out in the hallway. "What's going on?"

"Jenny's inside."

"Oh. Listen, I wanted to apologize for getting you in trouble. I mean, I didn't know I was, but I'm still sorry about it. OK?"

"Yes, well, fortunately it would appear that I'm

a better actress than you thought." She had no shoes on, and her toes wiggled in her socks.

"That's impossible. I think you're the best there is. I was just pissed off."

He stepped towards her, but she crossed her arms. "Why didn't you ring first? Why dash all the way down here without even knowing whether I was in?"

"It's like magnets—I can't help it. That's why I flew back to New York."

"Magnets?" All of a sudden her voice seemed to contain twice as many consonants as usual. "You weren't going back to Oxford, were you?"

"I don't know—I didn't think that far ahead. I just wanted to see you."

"I bet you didn't even buy a return ticket!"

"No, but—"

"You can't possibly be so thick—or if you are—" She shook her head as if to clear it. "How can you think you're in love, when we've work to do, both of us?" She had her hand on the doorknob. "I'm too busy for that sort of rot—and if you're not, you should be!"

Malcolm stared at her. Other people's outbursts of temper seemed laughably tame compared to his parents'. He didn't get what was going on and couldn't find it in him to respond in kind. "I missed you," he said helplessly, "and I think you're smart and sexy and I admire you. I can't just stop all that." He put his hand over hers on the doorknob.

"I missed you too." She put her other hand on top of his. "But I can't think straight around you."

"Me neither—that's why I want to be around you all the time." He moved closer and she came to meet him; then they were pressed up hard against the door, his hands were up her shirt, she was tearing at his trousers, and time went spinning off sideways.

"Sod it!" Emma jerked back onto the tracks. "We've got to stop doing this."

It took him a minute to catch his breath. "I didn't stick your hands down my pants! Why do it if you don't like it?"

"I do like it—that's the problem!"

"How is that a problem?" He tried to keep on kissing her, but she turned her head.

"I can't afford to get distracted by you all the time—I even fancy you when you're dripping wet!"

"Not all the time—we'll find our *via media*."

"Our what?"

"Middle road—my tutor's always going on about it. Derives from Aristotle's Golden Mean and the English disposition to seek compromise between extremes—"

"Aristotle! What has he to do with anything that matters?"

"The dramatic unities, for starters—"

She stroked her fingers lightly against him and he stopped, electrocuted.

"Does this feel remotely middle-of-the-road to you?" she asked him in a voice that grated like rusty nails.

"No!"

"Then don't 'wear your heart upon your sleeve for daws to peck at!'" She let go and twisted away from him.

"Emma!"

"And don't come round again—I won't buzz you in." She slipped inside and slammed the door behind her.

Malcolm wondered whether Jenny had been there at all. It felt no better than four-letter words to be sent packing with a quotation. All last term life had shaken loose his grasp of literature; now books were having their revenge, bashing his life about. He felt his headache coming back full force, and blue balls besides.

Outside, as he debated taking a taxi home, he caught himself listening for the ticking of a London cab's diesel engine, half-expecting a Checker cab of similarly bulky silhouette to pull up out of the past. The subway's speed would be less sickening than rush hour stop-and-go traffic, but the train was slow to come and he had no book to read, *The Faerie Queene* too big to bring along. Not that there was room to crack one open on the Lexington Avenue line—or even on the platform—at this hour. By the time a light shone out of the tunnel, he'd memorized all the advertisements in the station, and he knew all the ads inside the car by heart before he reached his stop, the din drumming all else out of his head.

Back home, he added more ice to his orange juice and settled down with Spenser.

"Isn't the heat working?" his father demanded. "Looks like a whole sheep's worth of wool in that sweater."

Malcolm stared blankly at him for the moment or two it took his mind to readjust to the twentieth century; he'd only been dimly aware of the front door opening and closing. "Heat's fine here, Pop, but not in England. You don't wear wool there, it's like going naked."

Mr. Forrester eyed the Waterford pitcher half-full of orange juice at his son's elbow. "Mind if I have a sip of your OJ? I think I may be coming down with a cold."

"And you want to pass it on to me?" His father had never been a man of much subtlety, and Malcolm resented this obvious ploy. "No thanks—get your own glass!"

"I think I will."

When his father returned from the pantry and reached for the pitcher, Malcolm intercepted it. "I'll pour—you've probably got cold germs all over your fingers."

"Thanks." His father took one sip, then set the glass down. "I need to change. Dinner date."

"Oh yeah? Who's the lucky lady?"

"Dolores Gottlieb."

"You know, you'll never catch up," Malcolm

told him.

"With what?"

"With Mother. At last count, she's got three exes to your one."

His father snorted. "Who says I'm trying? Unlike your mother, I'd rather learn from my mistakes than repeat them." He picked up the orange juice, twisting the glass in his hands without drinking from it. "What can I tell Dolores about how Nathan's doing in England?"

"Nothing! If she finds out I'm home, she'll sic Mother on me!"

"Point taken." His father put the glass back down. "But she's bound to ask me what you've written, even if I don't tell her you're here."

"So tell her whatever I last wrote." Malcolm was losing interest in the conversation; his eyes flickered down towards Spenser.

"That was two months ago, and it was all in French! I couldn't understand the half of it, except that it had something to do with that au pair we had when you were nine or ten. You must have run across her somewhere?"

"So I did." And enjoyed being reunited on a more adult footing. "*Vive la France*."

But his father was not to be put off. "Well? What can I tell her?"

"You can tell her Nate's been smuggling controlled substances into England from BeNeLux—but I doubt she'll want to hear it. She'd probably puke if you told her where he hides them."

"That's the best you can come up with?"

"No, but why don't you check your messages? I don't think you'll have to talk about her kid all night to get her into bed."

His father stormed off to the phone, leaving him free to delve back into Spenser. But he'd only been reading in peace for some ten or fifteen minutes—barely time for half a canto—when his father called out from the other end of the apartment, "How about mixing me a martini?"

"Do I look like a bartender?" Malcolm shouted back without stirring. Now that he'd reached the point where he was enjoying Spenser's epic, he didn't want to keep stopping and losing momentum; every time Britomart got pushed out of his head, Emma popped back in.

"More like a barfly—you need a shave. Might as well do something to earn your keep while you're here."

"What keep?" Malcolm closed the book. "You'd heat the place anyway, and you can't claim I'm eating you out of house and home when you don't have any food." He dragged himself up and into the butler's pantry.

"Not much point when I never eat in." From afar his father sounded faintly apologetic.

"What about breakfast?" Malcolm put in an olive and a twist; his father drank them this way at home, but not out.

"That's just for company." Mr. Forrester

reappeared, adjusting his tie. "This is good," he said after a few sips. "You been practicing?"

"Nah, it's all in the twist." Malcolm seated himself on the counter. "So who won?"

"I did."

"Then shouldn't you be in a better mood?"

His father shook his head, mid-swallow. "Straight sets."

In other words, boring: he was good enough at tennis to feel let down by easy wins. Malcolm watched him examine the olive before eating it; he had a feeling something more was coming, but could not tell what.

His father spat the pit into his hand. "Are you doing all right over there?"

"Sure," Malcolm said, poker-faced. They had stopped playing cards together when he, at eleven, started winning.

"Are you eating, sleeping, working, playing enough?"

Malcolm's perch grew uncomfortable; the jeans he'd found in his dresser were stiff as sandpaper. He wondered what vague sense of parental compunction—or perhaps the martini—was prompting his father to persist in the kind of conversation he hated as much as his son did. "The food sucks, the grades are in Greek, I broke my ribs, and there's a pair of local lovebirds who keep me awake humping each other up against the wall outside my bedroom window." He slid off the counter with a thud and returned to the library.

"What do you mean you broke your ribs?" his father called after him.

"Two of them," Malcolm shouted back—and wished he hadn't. His head still didn't feel right.

"And?" his father said from the doorway.

"I wouldn't recommend it. Hurts like hell."

"Are they getting better?"

"I guess so."

His father stared at his empty glass.

Malcolm said, "There's more in the shaker."

"You want one?"

"No."

He set his glass down on a coaster. "How did you happen to break them?"

Malcolm stared hard at the open pages. The letters were jumping like fleas. "Rowing. I caught a crab and didn't drop down fast enough. We went out in heavy weather, and I wasn't paying attention."

When he went off to boarding school, his father's parting words of wisdom had been: "Don't spend all your time cooped up in the library. You'll make yourself sick."

Early on Saturday morning Penn Station was deserted, the winos and panhandlers still asleep. Malcolm's parents faced each other off at arm's length, ostensibly there to see their son safely on his way. Malcolm, the son in question, sat on a pile of duffle bags and tennis rackets, wishing they hadn't bothered.

"You should play some sports," his father told him.

"You mean besides tennis?" Malcolm was good at tennis—though his father, after a few gin and tonics, saw something terribly poignant in the way his son's undeveloped body covered the court so capably.

Mr. Forrester glanced down at his son's skinny shoulders. "Try rowing. At least you'll get out on the water—"

"There's more to school than sports, Arthur." Malcolm's mother made a point of disagreeing with whatever her ex-husband said, regardless of how she actually felt; he, in turn, deplored the waste of a mind gone to seed in such a manner. "Don't crew teams practice at dawn every day?" She turned to her son. "You'll wear yourself out."

This was as pointless as all his parents' arguments: sports were compulsory at St. Andrew's. But Malcolm made note of his father's advice, having found that when he took the time to speak to him—less and less often since his wife's departure—it was usually worthwhile to listen.

Malcolm graduated from St. Andrew's six-foot-two. After the commencement exercises, he spotted both his parents advancing from opposite directions; before the ceremony, only his father had been in evidence, glancing alternately at the program and his watch.

"Where the hell have you been all year?" Mr. Forrester growled at his ex-wife as they converged on their son. He seemed underdressed without a wife on his arm: men of his age and income did not stay single long.

"Could we save the ugly scene for after the ceremony, Arthur?" Malcolm's mother didn't dress like other mothers, she dressed like someone in a magazine: hats and heels, slinky, shimmery things. The crush of parents parted to let her pass, sensing some foreign substance.

"It *is* after the ceremony—you're three hours late!"

"Really?" She adjusted the angle of her hat. "I must've gotten lost."

"It's not possible to get lost for three hours in Delaware!"

"It is now." She beamed at him, then her gaze fell on her son, who was half a foot taller than the last time she'd seen him. "What happened to you, darling? Was it something in the water?"

Malcolm said nothing, just shook hands and kissed cheeks as appropriate. He hoped his parents would leave before any of his classmates figured out who they belonged to. Boys his age tended to fall in love with his mother—as did men his father's age, and every age in between—and ask her if she was an actress.

"Congratulations," Malcolm's father said to him. Then demanded of his ex-wife: "How the hell was I supposed to file your income tax with you gone AWOL?"

"Congratulations, darling!" she said to Malcolm.

Then replied, sounding puzzled, "The same way you always do—with your accountant."

"You have to sign the return, Celia—and no one knew where you were! My accountant sure as hell didn't know, I didn't know, your son didn't know...I had to ask your goddamn husband, and he didn't know either!"

Malcolm craned his neck, trying to see whether his roommate had succeeded in spiking the punch yet.

"It's not funny, Celia! You can't fuck with the IRS—they'll throw you in the federal pen."

"I'm sorry." But when she opened her mouth to speak, the laugh escaped. "Artie—how you of all people could think my husband might know where I was—anyone would think you'd never been married to me!"

Malcolm's father looked as though he wished this were the case.

"If I were you, I'd have forged my signature."

"You can't forge your own signature!"

"Don't be obtuse, Arthur! You know what I mean, and I'm glad you did. I won't tell," she added, squeezing his arm. "Will you be staying for lunch?"

He shook her hand off to check the time. "Gotta get back to the city."

"What a surprise." Her smile broadened. "Where would you like to sit, darling?" she asked Malcolm.

"I wouldn't."

"How about doing it anyway?" his father said.

"Whose side are you on?" Usually Malcolm could count on his father to oppose anything his mother suggested.

"The path of least resistance. While you're at it, better bring your mother up to speed on a few more things—like where you're going to college—before she skips town again." He handed Malcolm an envelope and strode away, his footsteps visible behind him as slick, flat patches in the wet grass.

"How was your year, sweetheart?" Malcolm's mother asked him.

Malcolm pocketed his father's check and crumpled up the envelope it came in. He knew without looking that the Memo line would say CONGRATULATIONS, just as in November it said HAPPY BIRTHDAY and in December MERRY CHRISTMAS. "Same as any other: fall, winter, spring." The trouble with being rude to his mother was that she savored insults as a connoisseur: the wattage on her smile increased the worse they were.

"Is there anything worth eating here?"

"My roommate spiked the punch," he volunteered, having glimpsed the fait accompli.

"Thank god for that!" She straightened his tie. "What a relief to know you're learning something besides how to row a boat. Lead on, and you can point out all your girlfriends to me on the way."

This was the last thing he wanted to do; knowing his mother, she'd invite any girl he pointed at to join them and eviscerate her. "Who says I've got any?"

"Don't be silly, dear." She linked her arm through his. "Look at you! You'd have to do back flips to avoid them."

Now Malcolm forced himself to look up from Red Cross Knight and stare his father down.

Mr. Forrester saw how bloodshot his son's eyes were and sighed inwardly, but didn't press; he knew a brick wall when he ran into one and had not gotten as far as he did in life by pounding his head against them.

When Malcolm's father returned much later, his son was still sprawled on the window seat exactly where he'd left him, only now he'd switched to tomato juice and was sound asleep with his sweater, oxford, and T-shirt all untucked and entangled. His father thought he looked younger unconscious—except for the stubble—and wondered at his apathy; he did not appear to have moved since dinnertime.

For much of Malcolm's childhood this had been the norm: whole weekends spent with books on window seats, alone or with the girl from downstairs. Then in high school that all changed, and he vanished for most of his vacations, visiting friends elsewhere. His father attributed this sudden onset of gregariousness to hormones, and responded with a facts of life lecture, to which his son listened with commendable patience before replying: "They already taught us all that in sixth grade, Pop—except the part about paternity suits. Thanks all the same."

Was he now reverting to type? Whatever else went on, Malcolm kept on top of his schoolwork; and his father had sensibly opted not to try and fix what wasn't broken, leaving the prying questions to his ex-wife, who possessed no such scruples. Now, however, there was something about his son suggestive of a porcupine stripped of its quills. He shook him by the shoulder.

Malcolm came to with an effort and groaned at the cause of the disturbance. "Jesus, Pop—twice in one day? Don't you ever sleep? Or did you strike out?"

"I needed clothes for tomorrow. D'you mind if I have a sip of tomato juice?"

"For chrissake, there's nothing in it, all right? I'm treating a two-month-old hangover. Please tell me that wasn't all you woke me up for!"

"No. I want to know what you plan on doing at the end of the school year."

Malcolm was too groggy to register on the absurdity of such a question at 2 a.m. "Stay on at Oxford till July and row at Henley—or at least watch it."

"What about after you finish college?"

"I don't know. Maybe I'll be a bartender. I mix a mean martini." He turned away and closed his eyes.

"Seriously," his father persisted.

"Grad school, probably." He had not thought about it till this minute.

"What subject?"

"English lit."

Malcolm half-expected his father to object to this less than lucrative aspiration, but all he said was, "A doctorate?"

"I guess."

"How long will that take?"

"Dunno exactly—four or five years? You have to teach and write a dissertation on top of all your coursework." He propped himself up on one elbow. "Is there a point I'm missing somewhere in this conversation?"

"What concerns me is that you'll be twenty-five before you've finished."

"So?" This was becoming more, rather than less, unfathomable.

"According to the terms of your trust fund, you gain control of a quarter of the principal upon turning twenty-five, and I want to make sure you've learned what to do with it before then, so you don't have to keep on paying the bank six percent to manage it for you."

"Why not? Isn't that what Mother does?"

"Yes, but you're smarter than she is, Malcolm—you don't need to do that."

"She's not stupid."

"No, not stupid," his father conceded, "but if she won't put her mind to it—or to anything else—it doesn't matter how good a mind she has, does it?" He loosened his already loose tie further. "You at least appreciate the necessity, even if you find it as much of a chore as she does."

"I don't appreciate the necessity of discussing it right now. Didn't we already go over all that for when I turn twenty-one?"

"That was for your other trust, the one my father set up, and we only discussed what to do with the income, because that's all you get at twenty-one. Celia's family's lawyers didn't take the same approach, so I want to be sure you understand the difference—"

"Why do you know so much about it, if it's Mother's money?"

"I already told you—she can't be bothered. I still do her income tax, for chrissake! If she refuses to take charge of her own finances, do you think she's going to worry about yours?" He took his tie off altogether and coiled it up around his hand. "I may not be much use to you as a parent in other ways, but this is one thing I can do right for you, and I'm damned if I'll let it get screwed up by scheduling conflicts."

"Your feelings do you credit, Pop." Malcolm rubbed his eyes to keep them open. "But you couldn't have waited till morning to discuss something that won't happen for another five years?"

"You wouldn't have been awake then either," his father pointed out. "And for god's sake, don't sleep on that window seat all night! Go to bed, or you'll hate yourself in the morning."

"I already hate myself now," Malcolm muttered, but shuffled off to his room, cheered to think, It's not just me that's crazy—everybody else is too!

Malcolm floated up through layers of sleep anchored to the idea that if he bought a ticket to a play Emma was acting in, and sat in the audience, he could slip back into his initial stargazing state and walk out of the theatre unscathed. But when he broke through the surface of consciousness, the flaw in this dreamscape hit him full in the face: she wasn't in any plays right now. Even if she were, there was no guarantee he'd walk out of the theatre. He'd probably barge in backstage just like he did before.

He didn't see how ringing her doorbell a third time could improve things—though it seemed just as unlikely it could make things worse. Which left him with tomato juice and Spenser. Filling a highball glass he felt strange; it took him awhile to pinpoint that he'd forgotten how it felt to wake up not hung-over. Which turned out not to be a big improvement: not having a splitting headache left him that much more aware of splitting heartache.

A few hours into corage and guerdons, belamours and paragones, fowle gealosy and joyous treason, the sun swung round in a blazing parallelogram, baking him like bread. He saw so little sun in England, it felt like a long-lost friend;

he let it bore through his sweater and scorch his skin for as long as he could stand it. When the wool seemed about to ignite, he rolled off the window seat onto the floor, lazier than he'd ever felt in his life. Books were more fun to read when you didn't have to write about them afterwards. You could wade in up to the hips without stopping to sort everything you passed along the way into mental piles labeled "possible thesis" or "supporting evidence" or "interesting but irrelevant" or "for god's sake, don't mention this!"

He let his head loll to one side, fixing on the dark red and blue diamond of the bird's eye in the carpet pattern till it blurred, then sat up quickly and found it no longer pained him to do so. He twisted sideways to kiss the rug as if it were responsible, then kept on doing sit-ups till his side began to ache—but only in the ordinary way caused by too many sit-ups after a long lapse. He stopped and lay on his back a while longer, till his side stopped throbbing, then shouted, "'Arise, arise, ye more than dead!'" and put on gym clothes to run up and down the fire stairs.

Given crew season's relentless progress with or without him, it was depressing to contemplate how easily he was winded. But not as depressing as contemplating how easily Emma had slammed her door in his face two times; if running stairs let him forget that for minutes at a stretch, he'd keep running them, winded or no. When he was good and tired—for the first time in months—he took another extravagant shower and made two phone calls. The first number he looked up in the Yellow Pages, credit card in hand; he remembered the area code, exchange, and extension of the second.

"Forrester!" Coach Delaney sounded surprised. "Didn't expect to hear from you till August. You still in England?"

"Yes," Malcolm lied.

"You been rowing?"

"I was, but—"

"What do you mean 'was'? You won't win your seat back next fall if you're not in peak form."

"I made the cut for my college's first eight, but then I broke two ribs last term—"

"What'd you do—pull another Boris Becker at the net? Tennis isn't cross-training."

"No, I caught a crab."

"You didn't lie down?"

"I thought I could hold it."

"Always assume you can't. No race is worth that."

"I know. I was distracted." And it had only been a practice.

"So what have you been doing to train instead?"

"Not much. There aren't many no-impact sports."

"Don't they have bicycles in England?"

Everyone in Oxford had bicycles—but used them for transportation, not recreation. "That's not a sport."

"You never did like training, did you?" Coach Delaney sighed. "Listen, Forrester, don't go lazy on me over there, all right? Crew isn't just about winning races. What are you planning to do after you graduate? Quit sports altogether?"

"Not as long as people want to row in masters regattas. Or play tennis and keep score."

Coach Delaney sighed again. "Did they give you any PT to do?"

"Breathing exercises."

"Have you at least kept up with those?"

"Yes. They said I'd catch pneumonia if I didn't."

"This happened how long ago?"

"Two months."

"Look, if I send you the right exercises, will you do them? You should be up to it by now, and getting back on the erg."

"Yeah, sure."

"I can talk to our physical therapist here and see what she says, but I don't know how much good it'll do without her seeing you. You should get an X-ray first, though, just in case. Do you have access to a fax machine over there?"

"There must be one somewhere, but it could take a while. I had to go all the way to France to find ballpoint pens. I'll give you my father's fax number in New York, and get him to re-send it to me when I figure out where."

"All right. In the meantime, you can start running stairs—"

"But—"

"Forrester! Do you want to row for us again or not?"

"Seriously, I can't. They charge admission."

"Who do? For what?"

"The colleges—to climb their stairs. Everywhere there's a tower, they charge the tourists fifty pence a head to gape at the dreaming spires. I'd be knocking people over right and left. I'll run extra on the ground instead."

Malcolm spent the rest of the afternoon on the window seat in the library drinking tomato juice and reading Spenser, waiting for the fax to come through. The fax machine was in his father's study, but he couldn't settle down in there. Filing cabinets loomed in military colors—army green, battleship gray, fatigue brown; books had ugly spines as unappealing as their contents—Dale Carnegie, *Robert's Rules of Order*; the desktop bare but for a slide rule pencil holder, steel stapler with round head to pound, sea-green deck prism paperweight, and lethal-looking scimitar-shaped letter opener, its handle ringed with spent shell casings Malcolm's grandfather had collected during World War II. There was still a dent in one of the filing cabinets where Malcolm's father had hurled the deck prism across the room, its glass too thick and heavy to shatter against steel. There had been a bone-jarring metallic clash, then a non-thud as it came to rest on the thick Persian carpet.

Then silence, until Malcolm's mother said, straightening up gracefully out of a duck, "You could've hurt someone, Arthur." Her eyes traced a line between dent and deck prism, envisioning alternate trajectories.

Malcolm's father picked it up and replaced it precisely where it belonged on his desk. "No, I couldn't." His voice broke as he left the room.

Malcolm's mother fidgeted, as if she'd called a cab that was slow coming, and Malcolm sat still, feeling sick. His father could serve aces straight down the center, and the dent was smack in the middle of the filing cabinet.

He was about to give up on the fax and head for JFK when it occurred to him that he'd do well to pick up something to eat on the plane, or suffer the consequences. The only thing he could stomach at 30,000 feet was plain matzoh, so he went out and bought a box of Manischewitz for in-flight consumption, thought a minute, and bought twelve more boxes—cleaning out the store—which would hopefully last him till he figured out an alternative to English food. Lately he'd been having fond memories of the salad bar in Commons at Yale—not a good sign.

Back home, he found Coach Delaney's fax on the study floor. He groaned looking it over, but folded it up and put it in his pocket.

His father got home from work just as Malcolm was cramming the last box of matzoh into a spare duffle bag.

"I don't know how you can stand to eat that stuff, when you're not even Jewish. Tastes like cardboard."

Malcolm did not reply, so he went on, "That's more luggage than you arrived with. I take it you're leaving?"

Malcolm nodded and zipped the bag shut.

"Before you vanish again for parts unknown, would you mind telling me where you're headed?"

"Oxford. We don't get all six weeks off from crew practice."

"I didn't know you were so fond of jet lag." His father put his briefcase down to take his coat off. "Was this whirlwind trip just to get matzoh?"

"No, it was just to get laid."

His father reached for a coat hanger in the front hall closet. "Mission accomplished?"

Malcolm held up two fingers.

"So naturally you've been sunk in a decline the past two days."

No way was he getting dragged into this topic on his way to catch a plane. "Not my fault you came home early last night."

His father shut the closet door. "Since when does it take all night?"

"Since when does it's in, it's out, it's over get you gushing voicemails?"

"It's complicated—"

"The hell it is! If it were that complicated, you would have stayed in."

His father laughed. "You have a point. Well?"

Inconveniently, his father was standing between him and the door. Short of knocking him over—not feasible—he'd have to answer or miss his plane. "I was drying out, all right? I drank way too much last term."

"I can see that," his father said. "So?"

"So I won't next term because it feels like shit."

"The trouble with that logic is the follow-through."

"You should know."

"Yes, I should. So pay attention, or someday you'll be asking your kid to mix you martinis."

Malcolm was fairly sure he meant this for a joke, but with his father it was hard to tell. "I'm all right now—really. Just don't tell Mother I was here, ok?"

"I already said I wouldn't." His father seemed unaware he was the exception, not the rule, in meaning what he said.

Malcolm held up *The Faerie Queene*. "D'you mind if I take Spenser back with me?"

"That's what you've had your nose stuck in all this time? You should've been drinking pitchers of coffee! Help yourself." He stood aside to let him by.

"Thanks." Malcolm grabbed his duffle bag and headed for the door.

"Malcolm!"

"Yeah?"

"Go to the doctor, all right? Get those ribs looked at first. Don't just start rowing."

"Yeah, yeah. They're not so bad anymore."

In the elevator he wondered whether he was headed in the right direction; his reflection called

to mind a line from the play he'd first seen Emma
in: "Thou man of nought, what doest thou here,
Unfitly furnisht with thy bag and booke?"

Trinity Term 1991

"OH, YOU'RE BACK, ARE YOU?" TIM LOOKED UP FROM his pile of PPE books splayed out across the kitchen table. "I thought you were off globe-trotting again."

"Just to New York. What's with all the books?"

"I guessed right about your note. 'Yecuda' was my tutor calling. He took ill and canceled our fifth and sixth week tutorials, so now I've got to make them up." He started to run a hand through his hair, then left it there to hold his head up. "First it was the milk van out front, so I moved in here. Now it's the neighbor's car with the wonky gearbox out back. Have you got the time?"

Malcolm looked at his watch and saw that he'd never re-set it from Greenwich Mean Time to Eastern Standard. "Four-fifteen." He opened the tiny fridge and retrieved his orange juice from behind the milk bottles in front. "Why is there no decent orange juice in this country?" he said after a sip or two. "It all tastes like canned soup." He poured the rest of the glass down the sink.

"It's always tasted fine to me," Tim said. "Maybe you should have stopped longer in New York."

"No offense—you don't have Florida or California here."

"They do grow oranges in Spain, you know. That's where they come from."

"Then they must keep all the good ones for themselves and export the rejects. D'you want the rest of this bottle?"

Tim held out his hand; with his student grant stretched to the limit, he was not in a position to refuse free food or drink of any sort. "Have you tried orange squash?"

Malcolm made a face. "That's supposed to be fit for human consumption? Tastes like it's for poisoning rats."

"Did you dilute it first?"

"No. Does that help?"

"That's how you're meant to drink it."

"Think I'll stick with water." He filled a glass from the tap, but it tasted wrong. Subsisting on beer as Europeans had done for centuries—even if no longer necessary for reasons of sanitation—still had a lot to recommend it. "I don't want to lug a week's supply of Evian around on my bike." He poured it out.

Tim could no longer contain himself. "That's all you ever drink at home, I suppose? New York City water's not good enough for you either?"

Malcolm stared at him in surprise. "New York's

got great water. It comes down from the Catskills. Those are mountains," he added. "Come visit me sometime and try it."

Tim rubbed his eyes. He'd been at his books since 5 a.m., unable to sleep any longer. He could never make up his mind, even when fully awake, whether this American was insufferably rude on purpose or simply half-cracked. At present he inclined to the latter, took pity and suggested, "How about Ribena?"

"What's that?"

"Blackcurrant cordial. You mix it with water to dilute it. Then you won't taste the water. I've a bottle on the shelf I've been saving, if you want to try it."

"I wondered what that was—thought it might be cooking sherry or cough medicine." He mixed and tasted it. "Not bad—tastes like some kind of chick drink. Is it a vodka mixer?"

Tim stared at him, true to European cluelessness about cocktails. Then said, recalling the rate at which Malcolm had been drinking beer, "Just keep in mind I've only got the one bottle."

"I'll get you another—before I drink any more out of this one. Or something else you like better—more orange juice? Scotch? Beer?"

"You're not serious?"

"Of course I'm serious! What do you want? Hurry up and name it—the shops'll all be closing soon."

"I wouldn't half like to try vodka and Ribena."

Malcolm made gagging motions. "You won't have to worry about me mooching off that! I'll bring you some bitter too."

By some oversight, Malcolm's bike had not been stolen from the bus station during his absence. When he got back from the off-license, he parked it in the lounge next to Tim's, then took his carrier bags of Ribena and duffle bag full of matzoh upstairs to the kitchen.

Tim watched him fill his entire food shelf with the orange and green boxes. "Are you expecting a siege?"

"No, I'm expecting to be violently ill if I have to eat overcooked beef again."

"No danger of that till next term. Or you can always ask for vegetarian."

"Yeah, but it's always cheese souffle."

"Or eat pasta."

Which the Brits pronounced pass-tuh. "Not if they're going to put chopped-up hot dogs and leftover salad dressing on it! Is that supposed to be recycling?" He rearranged the Manischewitz to make room for the Ribena. "I think I'll self-cater this term. When the scouts set the dishes down on the tables in Hall, it's like feeding time in the piranha tank. Here's your vodka and Ribena."

"Smashing—thanks!" Tim cradled a bottle in each hand. "You know why that is, don't you?"

"No—or why the serving dishes are so small

they need refilling every other minute."

"There's only so much food in the kitchens. The faster you empty the serving dishes, the more refills you can get before they run out. All the tables are in competition for the most potatoes."

"Why? They're not that good."

"They're filling and they're paid for." Tim made space for the vodka on his food shelf among the cans of baked beans and spaghetti hoops and packets of Super Noodles. "How else can you live on two thousand pounds a year and pay ninety pounds poll tax, if you don't grab every stray potato you can get?" He filled a glass at the sink. "I've been thinking of joining the college choir."

"I didn't know you liked to sing."

"I don't, particularly. But my mate Martin says they give you tea and biscuits at rehearsal, and free dinner in Hall after Evensong. But that's not till Term starts, and I'll be lucky if I make it through the end of the vacs on my overdraft, even if I eat nothing but beans on toast—"

"That's ridiculous—"

"Complain to Maggie! Her brilliant idea. So many people haven't paid their poll tax, the government can't even keep up with arresting them."

"I mean, it's ridiculous for you to live on beans and toast."

"That's all I can afford." Tim poured some Ribena into his glass of water and stirred.

"You can't even afford that."

He stopped mixing. "What do you mean?"

"There's a reason rice and beans is the traditional subsistence diet. Rice is cheaper than bread, and dried beans are cheaper than canned—I mean, tinned."

"But then I'd have to cook them."

"So?"

"I can't cook. I tried to do a packet of Spanish rice once, but it caught fire and burnt the ceiling. Look—you can still see the black patch." He pointed to a hazy area above the stove.

"I'll cook," Malcolm said. "You just eat. We'll have a co-op."

"Can you cook?"

"Yeah, yeah. I won't set fire to anything, and it'll taste better than those beans in ketchup with the cardboard sausages."

"It's not ketchup—it's tomato sauce."

"Same difference. Here's your beer. I filled a jug at the pub."

"Thanks! God, I've not had a pint in weeks." Tim filled a different glass with beer, drank half of it down, and wiped his mouth on his sleeve. "If I'd got through these essays in time to go down the pub at all, I'd have been drinking scrumpy through a straw."

"What's that?" It sounded like the punch line to a dirty joke.

"Scrumpy jack? Homemade cider—cloudy, very strong. If you can only afford one round, you order that and drink it through a straw."

"What for?"

"Goes to your head quicker."

Malcolm thought this unlikely, but kept quiet.

Tim drained his glass. "I say, can you do bubble and squeak?"

"Do I even want to know what that is?" Malcolm's encounters with toad-in-the-hole and spotted-dick pudding were not something he cared to repeat.

Tim held out the jug of beer, but Malcolm shook his head.

"Cheers, mate!" Tim poured himself another glass and raised it to him. "I'm off home at the weekend, once I've got these bloody essays written. Come along, if you like—you might even like Barrow."

"How come?"

"Beer costs half what it does in Oxford."

Tim seemed so proud of this, Malcolm didn't have the heart to tell him he'd sworn off beer; he'd start training Monday morning.

"Why PPE?" he asked Tim on the train—the third that day: Oxford to Wolverhampton, Wolverhampton to Lancaster, and Lancaster through Grange-over-Sands to Barrow-in-Furness, the carriages fewer and older with each change. "That's what you study to go into politics, isn't it?"

"Yeh, generally." Tim lounged across the facing seat, the clothes he'd been studying in all week so rumpled it was hard to trace the outline of his limbs inside them. The straps of his canvas rucksack dangled down through the luggage rack overhead, and an empty can of Boddington's hung from his hand.

Had he not forsworn beer, Malcolm would have been keener on licensed buffet cars and trolleys dispensing drinks the length of the train. As it was, he kept Tim company so he could buy the rounds: Tim was willing to accept some form of hospitality in return for having Malcolm to stay at his house, but not to drink it alone. "Is that what you'll do after Oxford?"

"Yeh, I reckon." Tim nodded at the sweep of sea outside the window as the tracks traced the arm of a broad bay at low tide. "Morecambe Bay. All quicksand, and the tide comes in fast as a horse can gallop. Before they built the railway line to Barrow, people got stuck and drowned trying to cross the Sands—still do sometimes."

"Pretty, though." The sun bounced blindingly off the wet sheen of mud flats stretching almost to the horizon.

"Yeh, it's beautiful up here." Tim crushed his empty can against the seat. "So the Government bung all the nuclear reactors and toxic waste dumps in the North—never in the South, where all the money is."

"You'll fix that when you get elected?"

"Not bloody likely! Try getting Londoners to take you seriously when you've got a northern accent—they'll assume you're a half-wit the minute you open your mouth."

"It's the opposite in America." Malcolm hadn't thought too much about Tim's accent, except that it was mild and softer than the BBC or Oxbridge. "We hear a southern accent and think redneck." He closed his eyes, succumbing to the sun's heat beating through the grimy window and the swaying rhythm of the wheels on rails.

By the time they reached Barrow-in-Furness, the weather had about-faced to the point that it was hard to believe in such a thing as sun. Clouds thick and heavy as old army blankets spat out bursts of drizzle cold and wet enough to cause discomfort, yet could not make up their minds to drop enough for raincoats or umbrellas. Barrow felt like the end of the earth not so much geographically as philosophically: the town ached under an atmosphere of "Abandon hope, all ye who enter here."

Between the train station and Tim's house shops stood empty, churches were boarded up, pedestrians scarce except outside the turf accountants and job centre. The residential part of town rose on high ground; below, across a channel, sprawled a massive shipyard, half-asleep. The noble scale of the neo-Gothic town hall hinted at better days gone by; so too what was intended for a grand hotel. But the asking prices in estate agents' windows—even doubled into dollars—were absurdly low, the photos dusty and faded, as though nothing had moved in months.

As in Emma's suburb, all the terraced houses looked alike: squat brick squares crowded up onto the pavement with no front gardens, one block, one street no different from the next except for doors of different colors and incongruously recent vintage; Malcolm wondered if the owners had replaced the originals to distinguish each house from its neighbors, or if they'd all disintegrated with the climate. Other houses were constructed of a substance he'd not seen before, that looked as if someone had thrown handfuls of loose gravel into wet concrete.

"Pebble dash," Tim told him. "Cheaper than brick and lasts longer."

"Looks ugly."

"Feels worse."

"What do you mean?"

"If someone mashes your face in it. Here, see for yourself." He slapped Malcolm's hand against the wall.

With his rowing calluses gone, it took the skin off. "Thanks a lot!"

"You did ask," Tim shrugged. "Hurts more when it's your knuckles."

Malcolm wiped the blood off one hand onto the other. "That happen a lot here?"

"Used to, growing up—rough neighborhood. We'll give those pubs a miss."

There were plenty of others and no way to stop Tim—now that he could afford it—standing him more pints than he wanted.

The next morning Malcolm, head splitting, sat down to a breakfast treat that sounded as appalling as it looked: black pudding.

"Blood sausage," Tim told him, digging in. "Just the thing for a sore head."

Malcolm took one bite and reached for the HP Sauce, which at least would help disguise the texture, even if it tasted like a cleaning solvent. The English didn't seem to expect meat to be edible without it.

"This is gorgeous, Mum!" Tim shoveled in another mouthful of mushy peas.

"Have some more, luv—and do stop pulling your brother's hair, Deirdre!" Tim's mum stepped away from the stove to disentangle a little girl from a littler boy, her face flushed with the heat, hair frizzing. She seemed at once too young to have a son at university, and too old to have another still a toddler. "Sun's out—why not take your friend round to see the Abbey? I've still got the washing to do—no, Brian, you mustn't feed your bacon to the dog, there won't be enough to go round!" She snatched a half-full plate away from a curly-headed boy resembling Tim. "You can take the older two with you, and the dog as well!" She tucked her hair back behind her ears and scraped noisily at something sticking to the frying pan. "And you can stop moaning, Lily, or stay home and mind Deirdre and Rory while I'm at the laundrette."

Lily—thin, fair, and freckled, with stringy brown hair and marshmallow features—made what was clearly a rude gesture, though not one Malcolm recognized.

Enough of Furness Abbey remained to convey a sense of shape and size: open to the sky, grass floor flocked with buttercups and clover, the monks' medieval watercourse still flowing by, no place church mustiness could abide. Even Lily, after the ten minutes it took her to get over being a teenager, gave in to the urge to scramble over the rose-colored ruins, giving Brian boosts up and catching him when he jumped down, proving that anything he could do, she could do better.

If Henry VIII had not looted England's monasteries and left them to decay so attractively all about the country, would the Romantic poets and Pre-Raphaelites have acquired such a taste for old ruins? Malcolm wondered. He had a sudden homesick urge to throw a football around, even though he didn't like football and had no reason to think Tim would know how to throw or catch one.

"My parents came courting here," Tim told him.

"Shades of Shelley! He used to meet Mary at her mother's grave in St. Pancras Churchyard."

"Can you imagine taking a girl to a place like this nowadays? She'd think you'd gone round the twist!"

"Where's your dad now?" They'd got in too late the night before for introductions, and there'd been no sign of him at breakfast.

"Probably down the job centre—likes to go first thing, in case there's something new." Tim kicked up a divot with his trainer. "There never is." He kicked the divot again. "In which case he'll be at the bookmakers."

This, Malcolm had learned, did not mean a bookbinding shop, as he'd at first assumed, but off-track betting.

There was a faint tinkling tune in the distance; Lily and Brian came running, clamoring for ice cream.

"What d'you think, I'm made of money?" Tim demanded.

Malcolm turned out his pockets. "He's not, but I am."

Brian stared at him, confused, but Lily snatched the fiver from his fingers.

"Sorry for disrupting your day," he told her. "Hope the rest of it goes better."

She smiled as if it wasn't something she did often, flushed, and dropped her gaze—then bolted, tossing a "Ta!" over her shoulder.

Brian looked anxiously at Tim—who said, "Go on, then!"—and trotted after her.

"That's an awful lot of ice cream," Tim said.

Malcolm shrugged. "It's an awful long walk to take with your little brother."

"Yeh," Tim sighed, his accent expanding on its own turf. "If you've nowt to spend, you'd best bide where there's nowt to spend it on—that's Mum's philosophy. But when kids hear an ice-cream van, you'd like to treat them, wouldn't you?"

Malcolm nodded and referred the dog—a scruffy black and tan mix worrying a stick—to Tim, who wrenched the stick from its jaws and flung it far.

"I try to put a bit aside each term, but Oxford's so bloody expensive! Even if I stay on and work two or three crap jobs during the long vacs, it all goes for food and rent. But if I stop home to save on rent, that's one more mouth to feed, and no work to be had."

"What kinds of crap jobs?"

"Whatever I can get—answering phones, filing, sorting boxes in warehouses, hauling sacks of dirt round garden centres, refilling office water coolers...dead boring as jobs go, and not enough to live on—but we'd still be glad of them here. First steel collapsed, then mining—and now the Cold War ends when the only industry we've got left is building submarines."

The accounts of daring escapes from East to West Berlin that covered the walls of the Checkpoint Charlie Museum had not hinted that the lifting of the Iron Curtain could be as catastrophic in some quarters as it was a boon to others.

The dog raced back and crouched low, growling for tug-of-war. "Think I'll try for the Radcliffe Infirmary this year." Tim feinted left then right, dodging the snapping jaws. "If I can get something to do with computers, it might pay better."

"Do you use computers much here?" Malcolm had yet to see—or for that matter, need—one.

"No, there aren't enough to go round. But that's bound to change, so I'd best swot up when I get the chance. What'll you do this summer?" He let go the stick to turn towards Malcolm—then seized it backhand, catching the dog off-guard.

"Stay on to row at Henley, hopefully."

"And after university?" Tim lofted the stick end over end. "Row in the Olympics?"

"I wish! More university, probably." He'd given it no further thought since lobbing this answer at his father, but it still seemed as good as any other.

"And then what?" Tim whistled the dog back, and they started off after Lily and Brian at a slower pace.

"Teach, I guess."

"Is that a good job in the States?"

"Not really—nobody respects it. But it's what I'm good at. Literature, that is—I don't know if I'd be good at teaching it."

"Why not?"

Malcolm hadn't thought this through either, but the answer was obvious: "I don't know much about kids. College kids if I do a PhD, but by then I'll be that much older, so they'll still be kids to me. I don't have any brothers and sisters."

"You did fine with mine. Lily hasn't smiled since she turned thirteen."

"Terrific," Malcolm said. "If I land a class of thirteen-year-old freshers, I'll be all set."

Back from Barrow, Malcolm's ribs passed the X-ray; he figured if he could work his way up to training four or five hours a day, that'd be four or five hours less to spend thinking about anything else—like Emma. One thing Barrow-in-Furness had going for it: nothing there reminded him of her; not so Oxford. Her not being there to tell did not decrease the number of things he wanted to tell her on a daily, hourly basis; his heart hung heavy with the weight of them.

The rowing tank was next best to being out on the river, requiring almost the same focus; gliding back and forth on the erg mercifully mindless; lifting weights, less so, he could take or leave; and distance running bored him the way long division bored him once he got the hang of it. But he loved rowing, and if you wanted to row, you had to run. So he ran and enjoyed it as much as he would have enjoyed a dozen pages of long division.

Even so, puffing along out of shape felt better than sitting around getting more out of shape; and Oxford, embraced by canals and rivers, had more scenery going for it than New Haven, where he was unlikely to breeze by medieval ruins or gypsy camps. He was never far from water, the dirt or gravel paths alongside softer underfoot than street or sidewalk, with their own hazards: stiles to climb over, bridges to duck under, cyclists to dodge, horses hungry for apples in the fields nearby. Following the Isis to Port Meadow, he circled round the ruined abbey, and returning caught flashes of forsythia from the long back gardens of North Oxford across the canal, stopping now and then to lever up one of the footbridges so a houseboat—some freshly painted, some decrepit, some curtained and bright with windowboxes—could pass under, seeking a mooring. Closer to home, beyond Osney Lock, the towpath bordered fields run wild with daffodils, and at the other end of town, the winding course of the Cherwell took him past the University Parks, Magdalen Deer Park, and the shaggy oxen grazing in Christ Church Meadow.

Across Magdalen Bridge, down St. Clement's, and up the long, green lawn of South Park was the distant view of dreaming spires for sale on all the postcards in all the shops. On Sunday afternoons, bells from this panoply filled the sky with no tune he could recognize, but another kind of pattern he couldn't place, one that reminded him of an orchestra flexing its muscles—only the tuning-up turned out to be the concert.

He didn't mind every muscle in his body aching after a long workout; this proved he was alive. But running past the college boathouses marked how much he'd missed; sometimes, falling asleep at night, he caught himself breathing in time to the dip and flick of the oars he still heard in his head.

When it rained too hard to run at all, he hit the erg or explored the museums he'd neglected since his arrival in favor first of London theatres, then Oxford pubs. The good thing about English weather was that it never lasted long, no matter what it was. He visited the Pitt Rivers Museum in sweats and sneakers so he could cut out as soon as the clouds parted, not knowing if he'd have thirty minutes or three hours among the gruesome displays of shrunken heads and scant remains of the dodo that had captivated Lewis Carroll.

One rainy afternoon he didn't finish running until after dark, and stopped to tie his shoe on Folly Bridge before packing it in. There were black swans gliding down the black river, calling to each other, and he wondered why they had red beaks, when white swans had black beaks. It seemed wrong that they were not perfect negatives of each other.

The next morning he ran past the Post Office and bought a few red-and-blue aerogrammes with the Queen's profile printed on them in place of a stamp; for some reason she aged more on coins than on stamps. He took a break in the Botanic Garden to fill one out in longhand, read over the result, and realized it would be illegible to anybody else. Maybe that was why Emma hadn't answered any of his letters. Right. He started over on a fresh one, printing laboriously, and ended up with a much shorter message:

Dear Genevieve,

I hope you don't mind my asking you for a favor after only meeting you once. Could you please let me know if Emma gets the part in <u>Sweeney Agonistes</u>, and if so, what the venue is, so I can send her flowers on opening night? Don't tell her I asked, though—it's a surprise. Thanks very much.

> *—Malcolm Forrester (dropped in from London one night when you had errands to run)*

Fold in thirds, lick and seal. He crunched off over the golden gravel and dropped the letter in the first red pillar box he passed, before he could change his mind.

He bought a cookbook with rice and beans recipes at Blackwell's and made the rounds of the foreign food stalls at the farmers' market in Gloucester Green for the more exotic ingredients. Self-catering in Oxford called for a degree of advance planning unimaginable in New York, since all the shops—including supermarkets—closed by 5:00

or 6:00 p.m. Which was manageable on a student schedule, but how did people who worked all day feed themselves?

Measuring ingredients by weight instead of volume took some getting used to, as did switching from a four-burner gas stove in good repair to a cantankerous electric range with only two off-kilter coils—one large, one small. The other side of the stove top, where there should have been room for two more, was covered with a thick iron griddle that was in turn covered with a thick layer of rust. There was a certain amount of trial and error involved in keeping the rice from sticking to the pan, because what the dials said the coils were doing didn't necessarily correspond to what the coils did.

The first batch of unburnt basmati—to go with red lentil curry, Major Grey's, and cucumber raita—had the unexpected effect of luring Hadi out of his room off the kitchen for the first time in months. He was a third-year reading biochemistry, and as soon as the Radcliffe Science Library shut its doors for the night, he came home and shut the door to his room, leaving his shoes neatly lined up outside.

"I thought you'd gone home for the vacs," Tim said when he appeared.

"I cannot go home, or else I will be drafted."

"Not home to Iran—home to Sheffield."

"No, there is not room for me there any longer. My aunt and her twin boys now sleep in my bedroom."

"Sounds a bit cramped," Tim said. "Did they call off your Part I exams, or are you taking a break?"

"I smelled basmati cooking. It is my favorite rice."

"Good," said Malcolm, "then you can help eat it."

"Thank you." Hadi glanced at the dirty bowls and utensils strewn across the table. "Perhaps you would like to dine in my room? I think it will be more comfortable."

"Righto." Tim grabbed a stack of plates off the shelf above the sink.

Malcolm hadn't seen much of either of his flatmates all year, having spent most of Michaelmas Term on the river or in London, and most of Hilary Term in pubs, but apparently Tim had not seen much of Hadi either, because "Christ!" he exclaimed upon entering, "What'd you do, then, rob a harem?"

There was no furniture besides the wardrobe British bedrooms had instead of closets and a secondhand desk and chair by the window. Pillows and cushions were strewn across a crazy quilt of Persian carpets overlapping and intersecting in a maze of deep colors.

"Nice rugs." Malcolm crossed the room to see if they changed color from the opposite angle; they did. When his grandfather died, the appraiser had said this was how you could tell the real ones.

"My father and uncles are rug merchants," Hadi explained. "These are so thick and soft I don't need a bed."

"Should we be walking on them?" Malcolm asked belatedly.

"Yes, yes, rugs are meant to be walked on—this prevents moths. Just please remove your shoes first."

"Perhaps we ought to find a tablecloth," Tim said.

"Yes, a tablecloth would be a good idea." Hadi burrowed in the wardrobe, brought forth another rug, and with a flick of his wrists unrolled it. This one too had an intricate pattern, but no pile.

Tim set the plates down and went back to the kitchen for knives and forks. Malcolm brought in the serving dishes and there was silence while the food went round.

"It's no good your doing all the work and buying all the groceries," Tim said eventually, polishing off his third helping and downing his fourth mugful of beer. He ate as fast and furiously at home as he did in Hall.

"Forget about it," Malcolm said. "It's a waste to cook for one person, with such a small fridge. If you didn't help eat it, I'd have to throw out most of the leftovers."

"It's not on," Tim insisted, holding out the jug of beer.

Malcolm waved it away. "If I do bubble and squeak, you can help peel potatoes—or there's always the washing up." Though he didn't like to delegate this task, since the British didn't rinse the soap suds off before they dried the dishes. "Or you can chip in for the rice and beans, since you were going to eat those anyway. But I was going to cook anyway, so I don't care. Do what you want." He lay back on the carpets…maybe they really were soft enough to sleep on.

"I have some saffron threads to contribute," said Hadi, cross-legged and calm.

Malcolm sat up. "Really? Wow."

"Why?" said Tim. "What's so great about saffron?" He was lounging on one elbow so he could still manage the jug of beer.

"It is the stigma of the crocus flower," Hadi told him.

"And the most expensive spice in the world," Malcolm added. "Fifty dollars—twenty-five pounds—an ounce."

"And you're seriously suggesting we eat it?" Tim asked Hadi. "Why not flog it and eat out?"

"It is for a rice dish of my grandmother's," Hadi explained. "It is my favorite, so she showed me how to prepare it before I came up, but I have not had time to try since then. Now, perhaps, many hands will make light work. Did your mother teach you this curry?" he asked Malcolm.

"My mother?" He lay down again. "No. She can't even keep a cook, let alone cook herself. I just read cookbooks."

"Well, keep reading them," Tim said.

The first post the next morning brought an aerogram emblazoned with a full-color portrait of President Lincoln and another man Malcolm didn't recognize from any currency. He slit it open. Genevieve, unlike Emma, was a timely correspondent. Somehow her handwriting matched her hair: she dotted her "i"s with circles and drew hearts under her exclamation points.

> *Dear Malcolm,*
>
> *Of course I remember you and of course I won't tell! I don't think it's rude, I think it's romantic! Some girls have all the luck—especially Emma. She did get the part (Doris) and it's way Off-Off-Broadway at the Prince Theater, which is just a blackbox. It's not much of a part, but Emma says the cannibal island will be up on a scaffold, so they're at least taking a stab at scenery. Opening night is May 10, Previews May 8-9. Hope this helps!*
>
> *Love, Jenny*

Reading this gave Malcolm a stomachache. Now that his ribs were healed and he could train again, it was easier not to think of Emma all the time—but when he did, the prospect of not seeing her again dizzied him like the view over a precipice. Romantic novels he'd read by the Brontës and their ilk implied heartbreak was the direct result of melodrama; the injustice of it arising from ease, laughter, and good humor struck him like a stray bullet.

He could see no clear course of action, trapped in one of those standardized-test questions where the correct answer is D) Not Enough Information. If they'd really been having as good a time together as he thought, why tell him to get lost? Conversely, if she wanted him to get lost, why pretend to have such a good time with him? He could conceive of no innocuous way to pose the question, and this unanswered, what else was there to say? He could come through in a clinch, but knew no way to surmount silence.

He couldn't think what to say to Jenny either; some sort of polite reply was called for, but he could do no better than:

> *Dear Jenny,*
>
> *It's not much of a play, but thanks again for your help. Are you an actress too?*
>
> > *—Malcolm*

He also sent a note to Simon, the stroke, via Pigeon Post, asking if he wanted to do some sculling; Simon wrote back suggesting they meet at the King's Arms after lunch the next day to work out a schedule over a pint or two.

Simon was a big man with flat features and a mild manner, easy to spot in a crowd. Malcolm made his way over to him at the bar. "I wasn't sure you'd still be around this far into the vacs."

"Oh yes, still swotting away. I've got Schools in June, but I'm living out, so at least the College can't turn me out between terms for conferences." His hand dipped into his front pocket. "What'll you have?"

"Nothing, thanks."

"How are the ribs? Better, I take it?"

"I got the all-clear to train again, so I've been running like hell the past few weeks. I lost my calluses, though, with all that time off, so I wanted to put in some oar time before practice resumes—I hate starting off with blisters. When do things gear up again?"

"Er, I dunno." Simon looked away for a moment to concentrate on emptying his glass of Morrell's. "As a matter of fact, Oliver was working out rather well in the bow last term. He's got such terrifically long arms."

"If that's all it takes, you might as well send out a boatful of orangutans."

Simon's brows drew together with concern. "Sure you don't fancy a pint?"

"No, thanks." He knew Simon would assume he was broke; British bar etiquette meant taking turns buying rounds for the whole group you were drinking with; going dutch, bad manners or misanthropy. Malcolm had yet to meet anyone who abstained for health or religious reasons; the only conceivable reason for refusing the offer would be insufficient funds to reciprocate.

Simon ordered another pint for himself, and once it had arrived safely, said, "You'll be looking forward to Eights, then?"

"Considering I had to miss Torpids, yes."

"Right. Well, we'll see how it all falls out at practice. Compare times and so forth. Things tend to rearrange themselves somewhat from term to term. But I shouldn't worry about it. If it turns out to be a question of height, I'm sure you'll find a place in one of our other boats."

"How do you figure? Won't they all have rearranged themselves too?" Malcolm was liking the sound of this less and less. He couldn't spend his spare time training if he had nothing to train for, nor could he help how being on the tall side for life in general still left him on the short side for crew.

"Not necessarily—or at any rate, most likely to your advantage. Finalists are always dropping out last-minute in Trinity Term—I'm hoping not to be among them!—so you could probably stroke our second or third boat. It'd be better for your ribs if you switched sides again—"

"Yeah, but—"

"—and Eights is loads more fun in the lower

divisions."

"How can that be?"

"Because there you've a real chance of winning blades. In the senior divisions, most crews just row over or move up one or two places at best. But the lower divisions aren't as evenly matched, so it's quite possible to bump ahead all four days—or even over-bump into a higher division. It's a good deal more exciting to be the pursuer than to be pursued. Offense versus defense, as it were."

"If you say so." Malcolm stared at the blinding square of light that was the open doorway into Holywell Street. He hoped bumps races—where instead of trying to finish the course, you tried to bump into the boat ahead of you to usurp its place in the lineup for the next day's race—would not turn out to be one of those English eccentricities more appealing in theory than in practice. Racing other boats in a sprint race or against the clock in a head race, you knew where you stood—the faster the better—but bumps racing sounded more like a tennis ladder.

"Really, it is." Simon set his beer down. "I'm not just throwing you a bone—I've done it both ways myself. If you start out rowing on, you've nowhere to go but up, so anything can happen. But if you're near the Head to start with, you haven't far to advance, so you fret about falling behind. Particularly in Division I, with Oriel forever Head of the River." He jingled the change in his pocket. "Are you sure I can't get you anything?"

"No thanks, I'm fine." The pub was starting to feel claustrophobic with its dim lighting and stale air. Malcolm wondered how he'd managed to lose so many hours inside them during Hilary Term.

"Well, then, do you prefer mornings or afternoons?"

Now that he made a point of physically exhausting himself on a daily basis, Malcolm had no trouble falling asleep without downing several quarts of beer first. Mornings he didn't so much not want to get up, as not want to wake up: hauling himself out of bed was easy compared to how returning consciousness cracked him over the head.

His times on the erg went from embarrassing to discouraging, then improved steadily. But as the Easter vacs drew to a close, all the effort in the world could not alter the fact that Oliver Wells, though not the most alert oarsman, was six-foot-four with arms that dangled nearly to his knees. Malcolm tried to get excited about the prospect of winning blades in the second or third boat, but didn't know what he'd do with a painted oar if he had one.

As Trinity Term advanced towards Eights Week, his essays refused to write themselves any faster sober than they had buzzed or hung-over. Reading plays, it was hard not to imagine Emma in them, so he kept stopping and dropping to do sets of push-ups and crunches whenever his thoughts drifted off in that direction. On warm days, everyone alive was snogging on picnic blankets in Christ Church Meadow or entwined in punts along the river. Even on Sunday morning, when all the shops were closed, people still promenaded pointlessly in pairs. He'd never seen such a city for couples, and nowhere else had he been so aware of walking by himself. In New York he hardly noticed whether he went out alone, in tandem, or in a group, unless he was with an out-of-towner who could not keep pace: there wasn't time to stop and ponder, and no matter what you did, you'd never stand out among eight million people. But in Oxford even the winos in doorways or on curbs and benches slumped and sprawled with sidekicks.

It was halfway through Trinity Term before Professor Barraclough sent him to the RSC at Stratford-upon-Avon. Malcolm hated the place on sight. There were too many tea shops, and a Teddy Bear Museum. As a foreign student at Oxford, he'd never felt like a tourist; tourists rode open-topped double-decker buses in all weathers and stopped you in the Broad to ask where the University was, while standing smack in the middle of it. Here, the instant he opened his mouth, he'd become one of them.

He took an early train so he'd have time to visit Shakespeare's house and grave before the play, but the dank, dark rooms were as short on

Shakespeare's shade as they were on furniture; and the church where he was buried—despite the bust of the Bard with a savage tan—was just another damp, gloomy church. "What's so bad about leaving your wife a bed?" he wondered, picking his way through the wet weeds among the tombstones. "Presumably he spent some quality time there with her."

Only in the Swan Theatre did he feel he'd found Shakespeare: the actor, the playwright, the producer who spent most of his working life in theatres. Forget birthplace and deathplace and home and church. Whenever you went backstage or onstage or sat down in front of a stage, *there* was Shakespeare.

As *Othello* unfolded, the director focused on the fatal handkerchief as obsessively as the Moor himself did: each time it reappeared, it increased in size, till by Act IV it could have been a tablecloth—or bed sheet. Malcolm found himself rooting for Roderigo, the "sick fool...Whom love hath turn'd almost the wrong side out," a character too minor to rate blank verse; by the end, he agreed with Othello that the world would be a pleasanter place if the sweet weed Desdemona had ne'er been born. Before he met Emma, he'd never had a "type" or understood why some guys did. He'd always found plenty of fish, but now he saw no point in catching them. Emma wasn't the prettiest girl he'd ever slept with, or the lustiest, or the most well-read, but her mind most matched his, the way his oldest, favorite jeans fit best. When she seemed custom-made to suit him, why try ill fits off the rack?

Riding into town for his tutorial, he made an inconclusive scan of the sky for signs of rain. The fog hung low enough to top a few spires on the college walls, but had not decapitated any of the gargoyles yet.

"Fire away," Professor Barraclough said, when they were seated and supplied with tea.

Malcolm opened his two-ringed notebook and wondered why his handwriting still had the DTs two months after he'd quit drinking. He rubbed his eyes and began to read: "Although the main characters all die at the end of *Othello* in due tragic fashion, one vital question remains very much alive. Was Desdemona a slut or a saint? A minx or a martyr? Her own last words are tellingly ambiguous. She proclaims, 'A guiltless death I die,' yet when her husband twice calls her a strumpet, she does not deny it, but pleads with him to spare her life and banish her, or at least let her live one more night. Then when her maid asks who has killed her, she replies cryptically, 'Nobody; I myself.' Her own father feels so betrayed by her clandestine courtship and elopement that he is moved to warn his son-in-law, whom he despises, 'Look to her, Moor, if thou hast eyes to see; / She has deceiv'd her father, and may thee.' Likewise Iago, who has proven by his skillful manipulation of Othello to be a keen judge of character, remarks on Desdemona's precocious skill at dissembling: 'She that, so young, could give out such a seeming, To seel her father's eyes up close as oak—'"

"Yes, yes, that'll do." Professor Barraclough waved a hand to silence him and reached for his cup of tea.

Malcolm took advantage of the lull to check how the clouds had evolved since his arrival: the layers of gray loomed thicker, but the gaps between grew bluer.

"The intensity of your gaze alarms me, Mr. Forrester." Professor Barraclough's teacup clinked back into its saucer. "Have you sighted low-flying aircraft in attack formation?"

"Sorry, just checking the weather."

"To what end?"

"I was hoping it wouldn't start raining till after crew practice."

"Won't do you a bit of good, hoping. The weather won't pay the slightest attention. 'How poor are they that have not patience! What wound did ever heal but by degrees?'"

"You want me to take advice from Iago?"

"No, I want you to put your knowledge to the proper use you just did. Wilfully inappropriate quotations such as this one you very rightly objected to have no business cropping up in your essays, when you clearly know better. Explain yourself, please."

Malcolm closed his notebook, relieved he could leave off reading his admittedly contrived essay.

"I've never understood why all the characters in *Othello* are so single-minded. It's the opposite of *Hamlet*, where they're all so indecisive. So I thought maybe there was something else going on beneath the surface that I was missing. Desdemona in particular seems too good to be true, especially with such a yutz for a husband. How could anyone resist taking advantage of him? But she suffers from tunnel vision as badly as he does. I guess in that sense they're a good match for each other, but it seems like such a waste—all this talk of love and no one getting any, not even Bianca. Desdemona could have been screwing—er, swyving—Cassio *and* Roderigo *and* Iago, for all the good it did her not to score with any of them."

Professor Barraclough refilled their teacups. "I quite agree with you that Desdemona isn't one of Shakespeare's more compelling heroines. I find she pales in comparison even to Catherine of Aragon in *Henry VIII*, or of course Lady Macbeth—"

"There's a wife who knows how to handle her husband!"

"However," Professor Barraclough went on, ignoring this, "you must discuss the play as it is, not as you wish it were. Imagine for a moment that Desdemona is standing trial in court. What would the defense make of the testimony you cite?"

"I guess they'd point out that Desdemona's father and Iago are hostile witnesses."

"Precisely!" Professor Barraclough looked pleased. "And what character witness would they call—assuming she were not dead—that you could not possibly ignore as you've done in your essay?"

"Emilia, of course." Malcolm was starting to feel as if he himself were on trial. "But then the prosecution could call character witnesses against her. She stole her mistress's handkerchief and lied to her about it. Wouldn't that make her a party to Iago's conspiracy?"

"Ye-es, though her husband would of course not be allowed to testify against her to that effect."

"And her views on marital fidelity are unorthodox," Malcolm added, entering belatedly into the spirit of the argument.

"True. But what, in the minds of the jurors, might well override both those defects?"

"Well, she did tell the truth in the end, but how would the jury know that?"

"Consider the circumstances, Mr. Forrester. Her husband was threatening to stab her if she didn't desist, yet she still protested her mistress's innocence, in the process admitting her own complicity in the matter of the handkerchief. She had nothing whatsoever to gain by lying, and a great deal—in fact, everything—to lose. Ergo we can safely assume she was telling the truth."

"Yeah, I guess so," Malcolm agreed. "But we still don't know whether her truth was all-sufficient. Was Emilia with Desdemona twenty-four seven? She may not have had all the facts either. In Act IV Iago suspects Emilia and Othello of making the beast with two backs in Acts I and II. What if there were grounds for his suspicions? Maybe Emilia's defense of Desdemona was a smokescreen for her own offenses—though I guess no one would want to hear it."

"Not at all. I raise no objection to your topic, only to your manner of approaching it. You can make any case you like, so long as it arises from the evidence. But you mustn't suppress portions of the text to suit your theories. That's where law and literature part company. You don't want your scholarship to be 'mere prattle without practice,' do you?"

"No."

"I thought not." He settled back in his chair and crossed his legs, clasping his hands on one knee. "Talking of Lady Macbeth, why don't you have at her for next time? I believe you can catch her at the Barbican this week."

Bad news—or in Malcolm's case, no news—arrived early in England, to ruin the rest of the day. The postman didn't beat the milkman to their door, but he came close: when Malcolm went to collect their daily pint from the doorstep, there was the post—or lack of it—on the wrinkled blue carpet where it had slipped through the letterbox. By now he was sick to death of brown British envelopes and would have traded a whole year's worth for some red, white, and blue airmail. He'd stopped wasting aerogrammes on Emma and only asked after her in every other one he sent Jenny—which made half of them harder to fill.

When the florist in New York asked him for a message, he nearly reeled off the Wordsworth he heard in his head whenever he sat still: "Six feet in earth my Emma lay; And yet I loved her more, For so it seemed, than till that day I e'er had loved before" but realized in time that wishing someone dead on opening night was no way to win favor, particularly in light of all the sinister coffin references associated with her character in the play. Anything that complicated would get garbled in transmission anyway. "No message," he said at last. "Just sign it 'Son of Duncan.'" He'd have to ask Jenny if whoever finished the play for T. S. Eliot had done Doris in or not.

Dear Malcolm,

Sweeney Agonistes was awesome! Emma was a terrific whore—well, her character was—you know what I mean! She was hilarious, the whole thing was. Spooky too, with all those tarot card predictions coming true in ways you least expected. That stove of yours sounds awful! I'm glad we have a gas one, even though we don't cook much—I suck at it, and Emma eats for free where she

waitresses. Any flowers over there yet?
Spring took forever to come to New York!
I'm from New Orleans, so I'm used to it
starting much sooner.

Love & XO, Jenny

Dear Jenny,

I'm glad the play went over well. T. S.
Eliot must've been on a bad trip when he
wrote <u>The Waste Land</u>. No way is April
the cruelest month outside his old rooms
at Merton—it's a host of golden daffodils.
Too bad you don't cook. I went to Mardi
Gras last year, and the food was fantastic.
In England the most popular brand of
bouillon cubes is 'OXO'.

OXO, Malcolm

Professor Barraclough was seated at his desk sorting file folders into precarious piles that tended to slide sideways and collapse into each other. "Proceed, proceed!" He waved his free hand at Malcolm. "I seem to have mislaid my notes for the lecture I'm to deliver this evening, but I expect I'll unearth them shortly. If not, I've a spare in the sleeve of my gown."

"A spare copy?"

"No, a spare lecture."

Malcolm took his usual seat and began reading from between his cross-outs: "In Lambert's staging of *Macbeth* it is interesting to note, with regard to costumes—"

"Why do you think I'm stopping you?" Professor Barraclough interrupted, glancing at what looked like a take-out menu.

"Because that's a really lame opening sentence?"

"'Lame?'"

"Dull. Insipid."

"Well, yes, but can you be more specific?"

"No, I can't." That had been the whole problem writing this essay: how to translate into formal academic prose his gut reaction that three meals a day with Banquo's ghost would be far less frightening than three minutes with Lady Macbeth in the flesh.

"It is ill-advised to use the word 'interesting' in argumentative writing, Mr. Forrester. Why do you think that is?"

"It's too vague?"

"Yes, it is that. But a greater difficulty is the implication that what you are about to say is important simply because it happens to intrigue you. The word you want is 'significant,' which suggests that what follows will be of some value to others as well." He put the take-out menu aside. "Do you by any chance attend services at the cathedral here?"

"Uh, no," Malcolm said, "not usually. I went to hear the choir on Easter, though." Instead of gold or silver collection plates, the ushers handed round brown leather pouches with wooden handles and slotted mouths; he'd wondered whether this was so no one could see how much you put in, or so no one could sneak any back out. There had been a queue to get in, and in front of him a couple wearing those tweedy garments elderly English people wore; the man looked twice as tall as the woman, and they held hands through her fluffy wool mittens, pink-cheeked and patient. Malcolm felt they'd been specifically invented to annoy him: in New York he would not have thought twice about standing on line alone, but in Oxford everything occurred in couples.

"Just as well," Professor Barraclough said. "Last week I heard one of the clergy—I shouldn't like to say which one—attribute the current ills of society to a deplorable lack of religiosity. Such carelessness! I nearly left the Church for good after that sermon." He exhumed a teacup from the top of his desk and took a sip of cold tea. "Can you tell me why?"

"Because he used the wrong word?" Malcolm didn't want this conversation to continue, even though he knew the right answer; he wanted to finish reading his essay and get out on the river before the day clouded over.

"Which wrong word?"

"Religiosity. He said the opposite of what he meant. It's not something you want more of—it *is* an ill of society."

"Mr. Forrester." Professor Barraclough stood and loomed over the desk, his weight resting on both hands. "It is important that you know that." He waited a moment for his words to sink in, then came around to lean against the front of the desk. "Are you acquainted with the Martyrs' Memorial?"

"It's that tall black steeply thing with all the spikes, right? In the middle of St. Giles? If you tell tourists it's a sunken cathedral, they'll believe you."

Professor Barraclough sighed. "Yes, it's that tall, black steeply thing with all the spikes, and we were telling them that thirty years ago when I was up. Have you any idea why it's there?"

"No."

"Four hundred years ago bishops were burnt at the stake in this city over points of grammar. Punctuation was a matter of life and death. Language was a two-edged sword, and it was always kept sharpened. " He folded his thick arms across his blue checked shirt. "It is my opinion that the current ills of society can be attributed to a deplorable lack of attention to detail. What say you to that, Mr. Forrester?"

"Oh, I agree," Malcolm said, relieved the discussion was veering further away from his ill-starred essay. "Even the *Times*—*New York Times*, I mean—is full of typos, and it never used to be. There's nowhere to look to anymore."

"The current indiscriminate usage of words would have been considered grossly negligent in the sixteenth century. But in the present climate,

attention to detail is regarded as neurasthenic."
He let his half-glasses slip down his nose so he
could glare over them. "The kind of distinction
you just drew could have saved your life—or
lost it—in a more scholarly age. Remember that
whilst you're rowing!"

Torpids, in February—frigid and foggy—drew
crowds in accordance with the weather. But the
mass hysteria of Eights Week surpassed even
sunrise on May morning, when thousands of
undergraduates still stumbling about in the
tuxedos and ball gowns they'd worn all night
had thronged the High Street till no one could
move, craning to hear the boy choristers sing in
summer from the top of Magdalen Tower. Now,
three weeks later, the towpath along the Isis was
so crowded with drunken revelers and cyclists that
it was hard to hear the coxes over the din on the
riverbanks.

Malcolm ended up stroking his college's second
eight near the bottom of Division IV on the first
day of racing. When the starting gun fired, Nicola,
the cox, let go the bungline and called them up
to speed without a hitch. They held their place
unthreatened until well beyond Donnington
Bridge; then the race dissolved into a crisis on the
Isis. Just past the narrow Gut, Corpus bumped St.
Catz, whose coxswain lost her head and steered for
the far bank instead of the near, directly into the

path of the Teddy Hall rugby team's boat, which sailed straight on into Catz, causing them to sink. In the confusion, the following crews were divided as to which way to skirt the central pile-up. Jesus's cox took the high road, and Nicola took the low road, which proved to be so much shorter that they were able to pass Jesus and row over, finishing the race.

On Thursday the Teddy Hall rugby team crew, exhausted by the previous day's excitement, dawdled down the course in costume, clowning for the crowds until they floated past Donnington Bridge. They celebrated this milestone by stopping rowing, and Catz, in a borrowed boat, settled the score from yesterday by bumping them. This time both crews cleared out of the course without mishap, and Malcolm's boat was able to cruise straight by them without losing speed, Nicola urging them on to chase Corpus, who were now three boat lengths ahead. They pulled steadily and narrowed the gap until they caught Corpus to over-bump a few lengths before the finish line.

On the third day of racing, just past Hinksey Weir, Malcolm's boat was on the verge of bumping Trinity, when Trinity bumped Brasenose, who had been about to bump Univ: now they only needed two lengths for three places. "Next stroke, full pressure—go!" Nicola shouted. They pulled harder and narrowed the gap until their oars locked with Univ's and both boats could ease off to the side.

Later in the day, Malcolm watched from the towpath as the men's first eight from his college doggedly inched their way forward to within arm's-length of Pembroke's stern, closely trailed by Keble. He heard Clare the cox call for ten firm, then saw Oliver, startled by the airhorn blasts announcing Keble's overlap, catch a monster crab that sent the boat plowing into the riverbank so hard the bow sheared off and half the crew went in the drink.

Afterwards there was Pimm's and more Pimm's in the boathouse bar: Pimm's with strawberries and cucumber, Pimm's with champagne, Pimm's with 7UP—which the Brits called lemonade. Malcolm could tell the rest of the crew thought it odd that he stood rounds without drinking any, but they were not about to refuse on that score.

The first eight straggled in later, still damp, with Oliver bringing up the rear. "You were right," Malcolm told Simon when he got within shouting distance. "It *is* fun rowing in the lower divisions!"

Simon shook his head as he joined him at the bar. "Pity I can't say the same of Division I. What a bloody mess! We'll have to borrow someone else's boat tomorrow—if anyone'll lend us theirs after what we did to ours—or else make do with the practice boat, which, as you know, is a tub." He took a large gulp of his Pimm's Cup. "Well rowed today, by the way. I'll wager a tenner you lot win blades tomorrow. You were all on good form, with a perfect set from the start."

"That's what Nic said too."

"Good form counts for a lot." Simon stabbed at his punch with a cucumber stick. "I've been thinking about pulling together a coxed four for Henley, and Clare thinks she can do it. Will you still be around then? Lord knows if we'll qualify, but who knows when I'll ever have this much time to train again, even with Finals. Worth having a go, don't you think?"

"Hell, yeah!" Malcolm said. "When will I ever be living in England again? Count me in."

During Eights Week, Malcolm only managed to tear himself away from crew long enough to attend the OUDS Shakespeare production he'd been assigned and skim through a few of the books on the long list of recommended reading, arriving woefully unprepared for his tutorial.

"How did you get on with *All's Well That Ends Well*?" Professor Barraclough asked, pouring out the tea.

Malcolm opened his notebook out of habit, but there wasn't much in it: just notes and jottings that had failed to coalesce into an argument. "Not well at all."

Professor Barraclough peered over his half-glasses at the half-blank pages. "So I see." He handed Malcolm a cup and saucer. "Perhaps you'd care to tell me what your essay would have been about, had you written it?"

Stalling, Malcolm took a sip of tea and burnt his tongue. "I thought the director's interpretation got in the way of the play. They tried too hard to get it to make sense psychologically. Comedies don't have to do that, so why force the issue? This play revolves around the plot device, and Shakespeare stole that from the *Decameron*—only now that we all think he was the greatest writer who ever lived, we expect every line he wrote to be profound. But that's not what everyone expected in his day, so it's anachronistic to produce it that way now." He tried the tea again, but it was still too hot to drink. "What kind of happy ending is it, when a smart, capable, well-educated young woman tricks a self-centered, immature jerk into marrying her? Yeah, she got the better of him along the way and he deserved it, but now she's stuck with this schmuck and his child for the rest of her life! It's only satisfying as the solution to a puzzle—like those Gilbert and Sullivan endings where everybody gets paired off, but they're all the wrong age for each other."

Professor Barraclough stirred milk and sugar into his tea. He did not appear to be listening, but this was an illusion. Oxford dons had staggering attention spans and asked more probing questions off the cuff, after listening to their students' essays read aloud, than American professors wrote down in their comments reading them on paper; each weekly essay had to be defended like a dissertation. "You don't think this was Shakespeare at his best, then?"

Malcolm thought he caught a glint in his eye. "Depends what kind of best you mean. In this particular play I think he's at his best with what he didn't copy from Boccaccio: the low comedy of the subplot—that blindfold torture scene with the fake foreign languages—and the more genuine pathos surrounding the minor characters: the king's illness and his views on mortality—rather than the main action, which serves as an excuse to string together other, more interesting stuff." The tea, finally, was cool enough for a cautious sip. "To me, that's what's best about Shakespeare: how he could recycle a creaky plot into a full cross-section of life with characters and language both deep and broad enough to play at the Royal Court or next-door to the bear-baiting pit—and satisfy everyone from himself to the other actors to the Queen to the groundlings."

Professor Barraclough nodded. "Fatal to study Shakespeare and forget the groundlings—or the King. As a matter of fact, Charles I shared your view that the subplot of *All's Well That Ends Well* dominates the play. In his own copy he re-titled it *Monsieur Parolles*."

"Or the Queen." Now that it was too late to develop them, ideas were flying at him fast and furious. "I thought the whole play had a nostalgic tinge to it. The romantic leads are young lovers, but the most eloquent lines go to their elders reminiscing about the good old days and friends long dead, confronting illness and death, lamenting youth's folly and the changing times. If you take that to support its being a late play rather than an early play—and accept the later date of composition—then it was written at the very end of Queen Elizabeth's reign. Shakespeare didn't know that yet, of course, but he did know she'd outlived all previous British monarchs by a healthy margin, and she'd been on the throne his whole life. So I wondered if he might've meant it partly as a parable, or as a compliment to her?"

Professor Barraclough stirred his tea with his fountain pen, then laid it, dripping, in the saucer. "Go on."

"The way Helena's portrayed as so smart and virtuous and diplomatic—winning her way by her wits, an ace at her profession, vastly superior to the object of her affection—reminded me of Queen Elizabeth's position as a well-qualified woman doing what was considered a man's job in spite of the opposition's determination—and her own inclinations—to marry her off and neutralize her. So maybe you could read the play as an affirmation of her capabilities and a nostalgic tribute to the Golden Age they engendered—but also as an implied warning against what could have been, if she'd squandered her skills on suitors who were her inferiors. Bertram's personality has a lot in common with the Earl of Essex's—and it's not remotely convincing that any good will come of Helena's marrying him."

Professor Barraclough nodded. "That may

prove to be a fruitful avenue for exploration—but I'll leave you to determine that for yourself. Might I ask why you didn't write your essay on this topic?"

The English, Malcolm noted, had a knack for couching the most awkward questions in politest parlance. The real reason was he'd been too busy rowing. He said, "I tried to, but it started turning into more of a historical essay than a literary essay."

"You puzzle me, Mr. Forrester." Professor Barraclough picked up his pen and frowned to find it wet. "You speak as if literature and history exist on parallel planes, yet you're well aware that's not the case, or you could not have posed your theory in the first place. What do you mean by it?"

"Nothing—I just don't like history."

"No intelligent person can afford to dislike history!" Professor Barraclough's eyes blazed, and Malcolm noticed for the first time what color they were. "You can come at it however you like—through the arts, through travel, through politics—but you haven't got a leg to stand on studying literature—or anything else—without it." He took a sip of tea and made a face at the taste.

"History books are so contradictory I feel like I don't have a leg to stand on *with* it."

"Then what you dislike are historians, not history." Professor Barraclough stood up to scan his shelves, running a forefinger along the spines until he arrived at a blue Penguin paperback: *Life in Shakespeare's England*. "Source readings, Mr.

Forrester. If you can happily spend the better part of a year reading Shakespeare, I defy you to dislike learning about the Elizabethan Age from Elizabethans."

Malcolm opened it to the middle of a chapter on The Theatre, under the heading "Puritan Denunciation from St. Paul's Cross":

> ...Behold the sumptuous theatre houses, a continual monument of London's prodigality and folly. But I understand they are now forbidden because of the plague...and the cause of plagues is sin...and the cause of sin are plays: therefore the cause of plagues are plays...

Then flipped ahead to "A Dramatist's Reply to the Puritans":

> ...As for the hindrance of trades and traders of the city...that is an article foisted in by the vintners, alewives, and victuallers, who surmise, if there were no plays, they should have all the company that resort to them lie boozing and beer-bathing in their houses every afternoon...

He ripped out part of a page from his notebook and marked the place to finish reading later.

"You may borrow my copy till the end of term—though there are of course copies in the library, as you might have discovered, had you troubled to look." Professor Barraclough held the lid on the pot to refill their teacups. "That you did not, suggests to me that you've been making the same mistake as Helena, squandering your skills on inferior men."

Malcolm choked on his tea. "What men?"

"The rest of your eight, Mr. Forrester. 'Eight minds with but a single thought—if that.'"

Malcolm got a sudden, uncomfortable echo of Emma telling him they'd both got work to do. He cleared his throat. "Er . . . it *is* Eights Week."

"Quite." Professor Barraclough sighed and set his teacup aside. "I suppose every young man's bound to be Bertram one week or another. Mind you don't make a habit of it!" He passed Malcolm the milk and sugar. "Though if you're planning to stay on to row at Henley, you'll be able to attend the outdoor Shakespeare in the college gardens."

On Saturday Malcolm's boat got off to a good start, but veered suddenly to port when their rudder-string broke as they came out of the Gut. Univ were close on their tail, Brasenose having bumped Trinity out of the way in revenge for Friday.

"Stroke side, sharpen up!" Nicola hollered, reaching behind her back to grasp the rudder-yoke with both hands so she could still steer.

Malcolm dug in with the other three on his side until the boat's course straightened out.

"Even pressure!" Nicola called.

They made good speed through the straight stretch and were nearing the Cherwell Cut and the college boathouses when Nicola shouted, "Queen's are just ahead. Power ten in two! Are you ready? Go!"

The shell surged forward, and after six strokes the Queen's cox raised her arm to concede a bump, but not in time to stop the bow of Malcolm's boat from cresting over Queen's stern. The two crews disentangled themselves as Univ swept past, and discovered the damage ran to scrapes but no punctures.

"That's blades, lads!" Nicola beamed as they rowed into the Cut, out of the way of the other boats.

They sat panting as the remaining crews in the division pressed on towards the finish—observed with indifference by the one white swan and clutch of mallards bobbing nearby—and when the final cannon sounded, all abandoned ship.

Malcolm came up spitting and blinking the murky water out of his eyes until he could see as well as hear the riotous crowds on the riverbank holding high their cups of Pimm's punch as they swayed. From a distance it looked like the final scene from a period movie gone awry: straw hats and white flannels, sunglasses and sandals, Town and Gown. Children chased each other to the brink of the river, wildly weaving bicycles terrorized stragglers on the towpath, dogs barked, champagne spilled.

If this were a movie, Malcolm thought, now would be when the hero gets the girl for dessert. As he swam back to the boat, he hoped Emma would stick to the stage; it struck him that in Oxford tutorials—unlike American classrooms—it was the student who stood in the spotlight. Hands grabbed at him, hauling him out to celebrate, and he wondered how the hell he'd fit his oar onto the plane.

Acknowledgements

With heartfelt thanks to:

Kate Yonkers and Deanna Weber Zalman, the Best of 48 West; Tom Webster, for the Town to go with the Gown; Professor Geoffrey Hill and the late Canon John Fenton, two alpha tutors; Brian Bunge, Catherine Freiman, Olufunmilayo Gittens, and Lottie Labys, crew gurus; Jasmine Simeone, trans-Atlantic translator; Mehdi N. Sattari, for medical material; my long-lost cousin Gordon Hunt, for his tour of the family homes in Barrow; Stella and David Boswell, my home from home in Oxford; and my parents, who got engaged at The Elizabeth: *Sine Oxon., non sim.*

About the Author

GWEN THOMPSON WAS THE KID WHO ALWAYS RAN out of paper for writing assignments in elementary school, when she wasn't getting busted by her teachers for reading too much. This prompted her to earn a Master's degree in Creative Writing from Boston University, winning the Florence Engel Randall Short Story Award and the Lawrence H. Blackmon Book Collecting Prize. She graduated from Bowdoin College, where she won the Nathaniel Hawthorne Short Story Prize, and spent her junior year at Oxford, learning to put milk in her tea, drink warm beer, and watch as much live Shakespeare as humanly possible. She lives in Brooklyn.

OTHER TITLES IN THE
MIAMI UNIVERSITY PRESS FICTION SERIES:

Mitko | Garth Greenwell
Under the Small Lights | John Cotter
The Old Whitaker Place | David Chambers
The Guide to the Flying Island | Lee Upton
A Fight in the Doctor's Office | Cary Holladay
Badlands | Cynthia Reeves
The Waiting Room | Albert Sgambati
Mayor of the Roses | Marianne Villanueva

To see our complete catalog of poetry and fiction,
please visit www.muohio.edu/mupress.